Daniel Defoe

The Wonderful Life and Most Surprising Adventures of That Renowned Hero,

Robinson Crusoe, Who Lived Twenty-Eight Years on an Uninhabited Island

Daniel Defoe

The Wonderful Life and Most Surprising Adventures of That Renowned Hero,
Robinson Crusoe, Who Lived Twenty-Eight Years on an Uninhabited Island

ISBN/EAN: 9783337214012

Printed in Europe, USA, Canada, Australia, Japan

Cover: Foto ©Andreas Hilbeck / pixelio.de

More available books at **www.hansebooks.com**

THE
WONDERFUL LIFE

AND MOST

SURPRISING ADVENTURES

Of that Renowned Hero,

ROBINSON CRUSOE,

Who lived Twenty-eight Years

ON AN

UNINHABITED ISLAND,

Which he afterwards Colonised.

New-York: Printed by HURTIN & COM-
MARDINGER, for E. DUYCKINCK, & Co.
1795.

LIFE AND ADVENTURES

OF

ROBINSON CRUSOE.

I Was born at York, in the year 1632, of a reputable family. My father was a merchant, born at Bremen; his original name was Kreutzuzer, which for the fake of the Englilh pronounciation, was afterwards changed into Crufoe. My mother's name was Robinfon, a native of the county of York, and for particular reafons I am called obinfon, after her maiden name.

There were three brothers of which I was the youngeft: the eldeft was an officer, and killed in the wars in the Low Countries; and the other I could never learn any thing of. My father intended me for the law, particular care was taken of my education; but all his pains and expence were to no purpofe; my inclinations were bent another way: and nothing would ferve my turn, out at all hazards, I muft go to fea.

My father and mother were both vi-, olently againſt it, and uſed a thouſand arguments to diſſuade me; but it was all to no purpoſe; my reſolutions were ſo firmly ſettled, that neither the in- treaties of a moſt tender father, or vows and tears of a moſt tender and affectionate mother, could make any impreſſion on me.

I was now about nineteen years of age, when meeting with one of my ſchool-fellows at Hull, who was bound to London with his father, who was maſter of a ſhip, I acquainted him with my reſolutions; he readily promiſed me I ſhould have a free paſſage, and be provided with all other neceſſaries ſuitable to the voyage; and according- ly, without aſking any manner of leave either of my parents or friends, upon the 1ſt of September 1651, I took ſhip- ping for London.

Our ſhip was hardly got clear of the Humber, but we were overtaken by a violent ſtorm; and being extremely ſea-ſick, I began to reflect upon my fathers good advice, and the happineſs of a middle state of life, which he proposed to me, resolving, that if ever I should be so happy as to set my feet again upon dry land, I would return to my parents, and beg their pardon, and take my leave for ever of all wandering inclinations.

These were my thoughts during the storm; but that was no sooner over but my repentance vanished with the danger; particularly, when my companion coming to me, asked me if I was not a little frightened by the storm, which as he expressed it, was only a cap full of wind. Come boy, says he, turn out, a good bowl of punch will soon wash away all our frights and sorrows.

In short, the punch was made, and I got very drunk, and then all my former resolutions and notions of returning home vanished. I remained not headed for several days, until I was roused by another accident, that had very near put a final end to my wandering resolutions.

Upon the 6th of May we came to anchor in Yarmouth Roads, where we

lay- bound with feveral other veffels
from Newcaftle ; but there being fafe
anchorage, and our fhip being tight,
and our ropes good, the failors difpif-
ed all dangers, and were as merry in
their ftation as if they had been on
fhore ; but on the eighth day there
arofe fuch a ftrong gale of wind, that
prevented our riding up the river,
which ftill increafing, our fhip rode
forecaftle in, and fhipped feveral large
feas.

It was not long before a general
horror feized the feamen, and I heard
the mafter cry, 'Lord have mercy upon us, we fhall all be loft. For my
part I kept my cabin very fick, till the
dreadful apprehenfions of fudden death
made me come upon the deck, and
there I was moft terribly frighted.

The fea ran mountains high, and
nothing was to be expected but una-
voidable deftruction. Two of the fhips
had already cut their mafts by the board
two more had loft their anchors and
were forced out to the mercy of the
tempeft, and we, to fave our lives,

were forced to cut away both our fore-
maft and main maft.

The ftorm continued extremely violent, and in the middle of the night I
could hear fome cry out, 'That the
fhip fprung a leak! others that there
were five feet water in the hold! I was
ready to give up the ghoft thro' fear,
when on a fudden all hands were called
to the pump, and I among the reft.

While we were all in this confufion
and diftrefs, the mafter happened to
fpy fome light colliers, and fired a gun
I was not failor enough to know the
meaning of the gun; but I foon underftood it was a token of our extreme
danger, and I muft freely own, it is
impoffible for me to defcribe the agonies I laboured under.

Happy it was for us, that in the
ftorm they regarded our fignal, and
with a great deal of hazard put out
their long boat, and by wonderful pre-
vidence faved our lives; for with the
greateft difficulty we had hardly got into the boat, but we faw our fhip fink

to the bottom, and had infallibly been every foul drowned, if they had not come in that very nick of time to our assistance,

It was not without a great deal of danger and difficulty, that they recovered their own ship, however, they made a shift to land us at a place called Comet, near Winterton light house, from whence we all walked in a most miserable and drowned condition to Yarmouth where the good people furnished us with necessaries either for London or Hull.

I have often thought since, that it was very strange, that, after these great misfortunes at setting out, I did not with the prodigal, return to my father, who having heard of the ships misfortune, had all the reason in the world to conclude I had been lost. But my ill fate still pushed me on in spite of all the strong convictions of reason, conscience, and experience,

After three days stay at Yarmouth, I met the young man that invited me to go aboard with his father. I found

his face and his behavior very much altered, and I found likewife he had told
his father who I was, and that I had
taken this voyage only for a trial, in
order to proceed further abroad hereafter.

When the old gentleman faw me,
fays he, Young man you ought never
attempt to go to fea any more ; for
depend upon it, you will never be
profperous in a fea-faring condition.
Pray, adds he, tell me truly upon what
motives you undertook the voyage ?
Upon this I told him the whole ; at
the end of which he broke out into the
following exclamation :

O ye eternal powers ! what great
offence have I committed, that I fhould
take fuch a defperate abandoned
wretch into my fhip, that has brought
all thefe miferies and misfortunes upon me ? After his paffion was a little
abated, he proceeds, Young man, depend upon it, if you do not return and
fubmit to your parents, wherever you
go, the anger of God will certainly
purfue you, and you will meet with

nothing but ruin and difaster, until your father's words are fulfilled upon you ; and fo he left me.

I made the beft of my way to London, being at all hazards, refolved on a voyage ; and being acquainted with the captain of a fhip, I foon heard of a voyage to the coaft of Guinea. Having fome money, and appearing fomewhat like a gentleman, I did not go on board like a common failor, but foon got fo far into the captain's friendfhip, that he told me I fhould be his meffmate, and fhould have full liberty to carry with me what merchandize I thought fit, and to difpofe of it to my own advantage.

I was wonderfully pleafed with this kind offer, and concluded that I had now an opportunity of making my fortune ; and in order to my voyage, I fent to my friends for fome money to fit me out, who accordingly remitted me forty pounds ; which I laid out in goods according to his directions ; who taught me to keep a journal, and feveral of the moft ufeful parts of navigation. And indeed by his aſſiſtance and my own induſtry, in this voyage I became both a ſailor and a merchant. I managed my little ſtock ſo well, that I brought over with me five pounds and nine ounces of gold duſt : which produced at London near 300l. ſterling.

Soon after my return my good friend the captain died. Tho this was a very great grief to me, I reſolved to go another voyage with his mate that had got the command of his ſhip. This voyage proved a very unſucceſsful one. I carried with me about one hundred pounds, and left the reſt with the captain's widow, and ſo to ſea I went. But as we were ſailing towards the Canary Iſlands, we were chaſed by a Sallee rover, who in ſpite of all the ſail we could make, in a ſhort time came up with us, and now there was no remedy but fight or to be taken.

They had eighteen guns mounted, and we but twelve. However, about three in the afternoon we came to an engagement: many were killed on both sides: but, at length, being over-powered by their numbers, we were forced to submit, and all carrried into Sallee. Our men were sent to the Emperor's court to be sold, but the captain of the pirates, taking a particular liking to me, kept me for his own slave.

It was in this miserable condition my father's words came afresh into my remembrance, and my thoughts were continually at work to make my escape. My patron entrusted me with the management of his garden and house; and indeed I was not without hopes, but at some time or other, an opportunity might offer; the worst of it was, I had no mortal to communicate my thoughts to, and for two years I could find nothing practicable.

In length of time, I found my patron was grown so poor, that he could not fit out his ship as usual; and then he used constantly once or twice in a week to go out fishing, taking me and and a Morisco boy to row the boat;

and ſo much pleaſed was he with my
dexterity in fiſhing, that he would often ſend me with a Moor, his kinſman
and a boy, to catch fiſh for him.

One morning, as we were at the
ſport, there aroſe ſo thick a fog, that
we loſt our way, and rowing all night,
when it was light, we found ourſelves
at leaſt two leagues in the ocean ; however we made a ſhift to get to ſhore,
and to prevent the like misfortune for
the future, he ordered a carpenter to
build a little ſtate-room in the middle
of the longboat, with a place behind
to ſteer, and other conveniences to
keep out the weather.

In this he would often take us out
a fiſhing, and one time particular, he
envited three or four perſons of diſtinc-
tion to go along with him, and made
extraordinary preparation for their en-
tertainment, taking with him three fuzees, with a ſufficient quantity of powder and ſhot, that they might have ſome
ſport at fowling as they paſſed along
the ſhore. The next morning the boat
being in readineſs, on a ſudden their

minds altered : however, my patron ordered us to go out and catch a dish of fish ; for that he was refolved his guefts fhould fup with him.

And now it was that I began to think of my deliverance, and in order to it, I purfuaded the Moor to get fome provifions on board, and alfo fome powder and fhot to fhoot curlews, which were very plentiful in thofe parts. I took care to provide privately whatever elfe I could think was the moft neceffary, for the prefent expedition, being refoved to make my efcape, or parifh in the attempt.

When we were paft the caftle, we fell to fifhing, and ftood further into the fea ; and when we were got at leaft a league, I gave the boy the helm, and feized Muley by furprize and threw him over-board, telling him I never defigned him any harm, but that I muft confult the means of my own prefervation ; adding, that if he offered to return, I would fhoot him through the head ; upon which he inftantly turned about, and fwam directly to the fhore.

The action frighted the poor boy exceedingly ; however, I foon eafed him of his fear, by telling him, if he would be a good boy, and fwear by Mahomet, to ferve me faithfully, I would be very kind to him ; the poor child feemed wonderfully pleafed with my promife, and readily confented, and from that time I began to love him extremely.

We purfued our voyage, keeping ftill on the Barbary coaft ; but in the dufk of the evening I changed my courfe, fteering directly S. and by E. that we might be always near the fhore; and having a pleafant gale, I found the next day, by three in the afternoon, we were got 150 miles beyond the dominions of the Emperor of Morocco ; yet ftill I was under the dreadful apprenenfions of being retaken.

I continued failing for five days together, until I concluded, that if any veffel was in purfuit of me, I was got fo far to the fouthward, that they would not think proper to follow me on further.

After all this fatigue, I anchored in the mouth of a little river, but where I knew not, neither could I fee any people to make a difcovery : what I chiefly wanted was frefh water, which I I was refolved to go on fhore and find out fo foon as it grew dufkifh ; but no fooner it began to grow dark, but we heard fuch howlings and yellings of wild beafts and monfters, that I muft needs own I was exceedingly terrified.

Poor XURY paffiontely begged of me not to go afhore that night. The boy had a great deal of wit, for which, together with fome litttle broken Englifh he had picked up, I was mightily delighted with him : neverthelefs, the howlings and bellowings were fo very dreadful, that we had but very little reft that night, and to add to our confufion, we difcovered one of the monfters coming towards us ; upon which I took up one of the guns, and fhot at him ; whether I hit him or not I cannot fay, but he made towards the fhore and the noife of the gun increafed the ftupendous noife of other monfters,

The next morning I resolved to go ashore, and at all hazards seek some fresh water; the poor boy would have taken one of the jars, and gone and fetched some for me; but I refused, telling him we would go together and take the same fate, and accordingly we took our arms and two jars for water, and away we went.

I did not go out of sight of the boat for fear the savages should come down the river in their canoes, and take it away; but the boy seeing a vale a little further, ventured to it, and returning with precipitation, I thought he was either pursued by the savages, or some wild beasts; upon which I ran towards him, resolving either to perish or preserve: but as he came nearer towards me, I saw a creature hanging at his back, like one of our hares, but something larger, which proved to be very good and wholesome meat; and what added most to my satisfaction the boy assured me there was plenty of excellent water in the very creek where the boat lay.

In this place I began to consider that the Canary Islands, and the Cape de Verd could not be far off; but, having no instrument. I knew not in what latitude we ere, or when to stand off to sea for them; my hope were to meet some of the English trading vessels, that would conseqently take us in and deliver us.

The place I was in, was, doubtless, that wild uninhabited that lies between the Emperor of Morocco's dominions and the negroes: abounds with wild beasts of all sorts, and the Moors keep it for a place of hunting. From this I thought I saw Mount Teneriff in the Canaries, and tryed twice to steer my course that way, but was as often driven back, and compelled to seek my fortune along the coast.

One morning very earley we came to anchor at a small point, and the tide beginning to flow, we were preparing to go further in: But Zury, who it seems saw farther than I, desired me to keep out at sea, or we should be devoured by monsters: for Look yonder,

Master, says he in his broken tone, and see dat huge monster dat lies there asleep on the side of the rock. He pointed to the place, and I discovered a lion of prodegious size, basking himself under the shade of a rock; upon which I took my biggest gun, and charging it very well, shot at him, and broke one of his legs; and then with a shot from my second gun I killed him.

But the flesh of that savage creature not being good for food, I concluded this was spending our ammunition to no purpose. Indeed I thought the skin, when it was dry, might be of some service, and so I determined to flea it off, which took us up a whole day to effect.

From thence we went to the southward, resolving to live sparingly, upon our provisions, and to go on shore as seldome as possible, my design being to reach Gambia, or any other place about the Cape de Verd, in hopes to meet with some of the Europian ships, and if providence should not favour me in this my next resolution was, to seek for the island, and venture myself among

the Negroes; for without one of these,
I could have no other prospect but starving.

As we were failing pretty near the
shore, we could difcover feveral people on it looking for us. We could
perceive they were blacks, naked and
unarmed, all except one, who had fomething in his hand like a ftick, which Xu-
RY told me was a lance, with which
they could kill at a great diftance. I
was inclinable to have gone along fhore,
but XURY diffuaded me. However I
drew as near to fhore as I could, and
talking to them by figns, till I made
them fenfible I wanted fomething. They
made figns to me to ftop my boat,
whilft two of them ran into the country, and in lefs than half an hour,
brought me two pieces of dry fifh, and
fome corne, which was exceeding grateful to us; and, at the fame time to prevent our fears, they laid it down, and
went and flood at a diftance, till we
had fetched it into the boat, and then
came clofe up to us again.

Whilft we were preparing to return

our thanks to the kind Negroes for the food they had brought us, were surprized at the near approach of two monstrous creatures, which we saw running from the mountains in pursuit of each other, who passed the Negroes with great swiftness, and jumped directly into the sea, wantonly swimming about, as if the water had put an end to their fury ; at last one of them com-

ing nearer to the boat, than I defired,
I took one of the guns and let fly at
him, and killed him.

I cannot exprefs the confternation of
the poor Negroes, upon hearing the
report of the gun, nor their furprife
at feeing the creature flain by it.   I
made figns to them to draw it out of
the water by a rope, which they accordingly did, and then perceived it
was a beautiful leopard, which made
me defirous of the fkin : and the Negroes being no lefs defirous of the flefh,
I freely gave it them ; as for the other,
which was likewife a leopard, it made
back to the mountaius with prodigious
fwiftnefs.

The Negroes having furnifhed us
with the beft provifions which the nature of their country and circumftances would allow, I took my leave of
them, and in eleven days fail I came in
fight of Cape de Verd, or thofe Iflands
that go by that name, but could not
by any means reach either of them : u-
pon which I grew extremely dejected ;
when XURY, with a fort of terror cried

out, Mastro, Mastro, a great ship
vid a sail. I ſoon perceived ſhe was a
Portugueze, and, as I conjectured,
bound to Guinea for negroes, upon
which I ſtrove all that I could to come
up with them ; but all my ſtriving had
been in vain, if they had not happened
to ſpy me, and ſhortened their ſails to
ſtop for me.

Encouraged by this, I ſet up my an-
cient, and fired a gun in token of diſtreſs, upon which they kindly lay by,
till I came up with them. It happened
there was a Scotch Sailor on board, to
whom I made my caſe known, and then
they took me into their ſhip.

You may well imagine my joy was
exceeding great for this unexpected deliverance, eſpecially when I found the
Captain of the ſhip was very kind and
compaſſionate to me ; to whom in return for his friendſhip, I offered all I
had, which he as generouſly refuſed ?
telling me, his Chriſtian charity taught
taught him better. Thoſe effects you
have, ſays he, will be a means to ſup-

port you when you come to the Brazils, and provide for your paſſage home to your native country; and indeed he acted with ſtrict juſtice towards me in all reſpects.

He bought my boat of me, and gave me his note to pay me eighty pieces of eight for it, when we came to the Brazels. He gave me alſo ſixty for my boy Xury, whom I did not part with without ſome reluctancy : however, the boy being willing, I agreed he ſhould be ſet at liberty after ten years ſervice.

We arrived at the bay of All-Saints, after twenty-two days ſail. The good man would not take any thing for my paſſage. He gave me twenty ducats for the leopard ſkin, and forty for the lion's ; every thing he cauſed to be delivered, and what I would ſell he bought in ſhort I made 220 pieces of my cargo, and with this little ſtock I began as it were, to enter anew into the world.

He recommended me to an honeſt planter, with whom I lived in the nature of a ſervent, till I had informed myſelf ſomething in the manner of planting and making ſugar ; and obſerving the great advantages of that buſineſs, I reſolved to get the money I had left behind me in England remitted, and to buy a plantation.

In ſhort, I purchaſed a plantation adjoining to that of an honeſt Portugueze born of Engliſh parents, whom upon all occaſions I found a very kind and uſeful neighbour. Our ſtocks at firſt were both very low ; neverthelefs by our induſtry and care, in a ſhort time we made conſiderable improvements, and began to grow rich. And now it was I repented the loſs of my dear boy XURY, having no mortal to aſſiſt me, nor no body to converſe with but my neighbour only.

I was in ſome meaſure ſettled before the Captain that took me up left the Braſils. One day I went to him, and told him what ſtock I had left in London, and deſired his aſſiſtance in getting a remittance, to which the good gentleman replied, he would only have me ſend for half, left it ſhould miſcarry and, if it did, the reſt would ſup-

ply me ; and so, taking letters of pro-
curation from me, he assured me he
would serve me with the utmost of his
power ; and in truth he kept his word
with me, and was extremely kind to
me upon all occasions.

And now my wealth began to increase
apace ; and, even in this state I might
have been happy enough, if my ambi-
tion and roving inclination had not had
too great a power over me. I had now
lived four years in the Brasils, and had
not only learned the language, but con-
tracted an acquaintence with several of
the most eminent merchants at St. Sal-
vadore, to whom relating the manner
of my two voyages to Guinea, and the
great advantages of trading to those
parts, they gave such earnest attention
to what I said, that three of them came
to me, and told me, they had a mind
to fit out a ship to go to Guinea, and
if I would go their supercargo, and
manage the trade, I should have a
fourth part without putting in any stock.

This I took to be a fair proposal :
and, upon condition they would look

after my plantation in my abfence, I
confented to it ; and accordingly a fhip
being fitted out, and all things in rea-
dinefs, we fet fail the firft of September
1659, fteering northward upon the coaft,
in order to gain the coaft of Africa :
but we had not failed many days before
we were overtaken by a violent ftorm,
which lafted twelve days fucceffively ;
when the weather cleared up we found
ourfelves in eleven degrees of north-
latitude, upon the coaft of Guinea ;
upon which the captain gave reafons
for returning, which I oppofed, coun-
felling him rather to ftand for Barbadoes where I judged we might arrive
in fifteen days ; fo altering our courfe
fteering weftward in order to reach the
Leward Iflands ; and were here overtaken by a terrible tempeft.

In this great diftrefs, one of our men
cried out land, land ! when looking
out that very moment we found our
fhip was ftruck upon the fand, and expected we would fink, and that we
fhould immediately all be loft. We

knew not where we were driven, and
what was worfe, the fhip was unable
to hold out many moments longer.

Whilft we were looking upon one
another, expecting death every moment, the mate, affifted by the crew,
hauled out the long boat ; and eleven
of us omitted ourfelves to the fury of
the fea and God's mercy. But the
tempeft was fo violent, and the fea ran
fo high, that it was impoffible for the
boat to live. When we had been driven about a league, comes a prodigious wave aftern of us, and overfet us
in an inftant ; fo that we hardly had
time to call upon God to receive our
fouls.

When men are ftrugling with the pangs
of death, they are commonly infenfi-
ble ; but the cafe was quite different
with me : for while I was overwhelm-
ed with the water, I had the moft
dreadful apprehenfions ; and the joys
of heaven and the torments of hell
were alternately in my thoughts, and
yet ftill I kept ftriving on, while all
my companions were loft, till the wave

had fpent itfelf, and retiring had thrown me upon the fhore half dead with the great quantity of water I had taken in during my ftrugglings ; however I got upon my feet as faft as I could, left another wave fhould carry me back ; but notwithftanding I made all the fpeed I could, yet another wave came which dafhed me againft a piece of rock, in fuch a furious manner that it made me fenfelefs. However, recovering a little before the return of the next wave, which would doubtlefs have carried me off, I held faft hold of the rock, till the fucceeding wave abated, and then I made fhift to reach the main land, where tired and almoft fpent I fat down upon the fhore, contemplating the manner of my prefent prefervation.

After I had returned thanks to Almighty God for this wonderful prefervation, I began to look about me, to confider what a place I was in, and what was next to be done, in order to my fortune fubfiftence. I could neither fee houfe nor people ; wet and

hungary, and yet had nothing to help
me, not fo much as a weapon to defend me againft the wild beafts. In
fhort, I had nothing in the world but
a knife, a fhort tobacco pipe, and a
box half full of tobacco ; and, what
was worfe, night coming on, I was
under the moft dreadful apprehenfions
of being devoured by wild beafts, that
I heard howling and roaring about me ;
fo that I had no profpect, but to expect another kind of death more terrible than that I had fo lately efcaped.
In this diftrefs I walked about a furlong
into the country, to feek frefh water,
which I luckily happened upon ; fo taking a tree, where I feated myfelf fo
t   I could not fall, and there I fell
afleep till morning.

It was day light before I left my ap-
partment in the tree, when coming
down, and looking round, I perceived
that the tempeft was ceafed, and that
the fhip was driven to the rock where
I efcaped ; and, looking further, I faw
the fhip's boat lying about a mile to

the right, where the waves had cast her up.

I hoped to have got to the boat, but the water between that and the shore rendered that impractible ; so that I returned again towards the ship, in hopes to get something from thence for my present subsistence.

At all hazards I resolved to get to the ship, and so stripping, leaded into the water, and swimming around her, I had the good fortune to spy a rope hanging so low down, that I could reach it, by the help of which, with some difficulty, I got into the fore-castle. Here I found that the ship was bulged, her head lifted up against a bank, and her stern almost in the water ; all her quarter, and what was there, was free and dry ; and I found the provisions in good order, and wanted for nothing but a boat to carry what I had occasion for.

Necessity which is the mother of invention, put a prospect into my head. There was on board several spare yards, a spare top-mast or two, and three

large fpars of wood ; with thefe I fell
to work, flinging as many of them o-
verboard as I could manage, and tied
them together, that they might not
drive away. When this was done, I
tied them together in the form of a
raft, and laid three or four fhort pieces of plank upon them crofs ways. I
found it would bear me, but a very little weight befides ! and fo to ftrength-
en my raft, I cut a topmaft into three
or four lengths, and added them to it,
and then I confidered what was moft
proper to load with, it being then ca-
pable to carry a tollarable weight.

At firft I laid upon it all the boards
I could get, and then I lowered down
three of the feamens chefts, and filled
them with provifions of all forts; I found
cloth enough, but then I took no more
than my prefent occafions required.

My concern was chiefly upon tools
to work with, and fire arms and ammunition ; and accordingly, I found in my
fearch, the carpenter's cheft, and in the
great cabin fome fire arms and ammunition; all which I put aboard my raft

and ſo with two broken oars, &c. I put
to ſea.

Though every thing at firſt ſeemed
to favour my deſign : yet after I had
ſailed adout a mile, I found, on a ſudden, the fore part of my raft run a-
ground, ſo that it was with the greateſt difficulty imaginable I kept my cargo right together ; and indeed, if I
had not been extreemly diligent and
careful, all had been loſt, and ſunk into the ſea ; but, after ſome time, Providence ſo ordered it, and by the riſ-
ing of the water, my raft floated a-
gain, and ſo I happily landed my effect.

Not far from the place where I landed, which was at the mouth of a little
cove, I diſcovered a very high hill ſur-
rounded with a great many little ones,
and thither I was reſolved to go and
view the country, and ſee what place
was proper for me to fix my habitation in ; and accordingly, armed myſelf with a fowling-piece, and piſtol,
and ſome ammunition. I aſcended the
mountains to ſee ; and there I found I

was in an island surrounded by the sea:
it seemed to be a barren uncultivated
country, and only inhabited by wild
beasts.

Returning afterwards to my raft, I
got my goods on shore, and being very much afraid of the wild beasts, I
made sort of a fence or barricade about
it, which I thought might in some measure, secure me against the dangers
that I was apprehensive of ; and so that
night I slept very comfortably ; and
next morning, when I awaked, resolved, to again to the ship to get such further necessaries, as I had most occasion
for, before another storm came, when
I knew she must be dashed to pieces.

In order to this second expedition, I
mended my raft, where I found it de-
fective, and brought away from the ship
a great many other tools, clothes ammunition, and whatever else I thought
most necessary for my future preservation and subsistence ; and when I had
picked up every thing I could, I made
haste to shore, fearing the wild beasts

might come and devour what I had already landed.

When I had landed the second cargo I fell immediately to work to make me a little tent, and fortified it in the beft manner I could, to fecure myfelf, as much as poffible, againft any fudden attempt, either from man or beaft: after this I charged my fire arms, blocked up the doors, and laid the bed I had brought from the fhip upon the ground, and flept as comfortably, as though I had been in my native country.

But ftill the thoughts of my future fubfiftance and prefervation were uppermoft in my thoughts, and therefore I went to the fhip as often as poffible, and brought away every thing I thought could be of any ufe; and, indeed, had fo ftored myfelf, that I judged I was tolerably provided for a confiderable time.

I had now been eleven days in this ifland, and as many days on board of the fhip; as I was going the twelfth

C

time, the wind began to rise; however, I ventured at low water, and with some difficulty reaching the ship, and rummaging the cabins, I found several other neceffaries, and, among other things, about thirty-fix pounds fterling in pieces of eight, which, confidering my prefent circumftances, I concluded was of fmall value : however, I wrapped it up in a canvafs bag, and perceiving the ftorm began to increafe, with all that I was able to carry with me, I made the beft of my way to the fhore.

That night I flept very contentedly in my little fortification ; but when I looked out in the morning, I found that the fhip was loft. I was much concerned at this in my thoughts; but when I reflected I had done every thing in my power to recover what was ufeful for me, I comforted myfelf in the beft manner I could, and fubmitted entirely to the will of Providence.

And now my thoughts were wholly taken up how to defend and preferve myfelf from the favages and wild beafts, which I was extremely apprehenfive might be in some part or other of this island; and at one time I thought to dig me a cave, at another to build me a tent; at length I resolved to do both, and contrived it in the following manner.

I considered the ground where I was, was moorish, and that I had no convenience of fresh water; and therefore I determined to find out a place more healthful and convenient; and, to my great comfort and satisfaction, I soon found one that answered my expectation.

The place was a little plain, near a rising hill; the front being as steep as the side of a house: on the side of this rock was a little hollow place resembling the entrance of a cave: just before this place I resolved my tent should stand. This plain was a hundred yards broad, and twice as long, with a pleasant descent every way to the sea side. After this I drew a semi-circle, containing about two yards in the diameter; and when that was done, I drove a row of stakes not above six inches fortification, which I concluded was in a great measure impregnable against any sudden attempts either of savages or wild beasts: and, for my better security, I would have no doors, but came out and in by the help of a ladder, which I made for that purpose.

Into this little garrison I carried all my stores and ammunition, and afterwards continued to work: I not only made me a little cellar, but likewise made my fortification stronger by the earth and stones I dug out of the rock. One day a shower of rain falling, attended with thunder and lightning, I was under terrible apprehensions lest it should take fire, and not only hinder me from killing fowls, which was necessary subsistence, but likewise blow up me and my garrison at once; the quantity I had by me consisting of 150 pound weight at least. Having thus established myself as king of the island,

I went every day out with my gun to
see what I could kill that was fit to eat,
and soon perceived there were great
numbers of goats, but they were shy;
however, watching them very narrow-
ly, I happened to shoot a she goat as
she was suckling her young one, which
not thinking her dam killed, followed
me home to my enclosure. I lifted the
kid over the pales, and would willingly
have kept it alive, but the poor creature refusing to eat, I was forced to kill
it for my subsistence.

Thus entering into an odd state, of
life as ever befel any unfortunate man,
I was continually reflecting on the mi-
sery of my condition; till at length
considering there was no remedy, and
that I was obliged to make the best of
a bad market : and withal, reflecting
upon the many turns of Providence in
my particular preservation, I grew
more sedate and temperate.

As near as my account would serve
me, it was the 30th day of September
when I first landed upon this desolate
island ; but I was at a great loss for pen

ink, and paper, to keep a register of time, and even the remembrance of the Sabbath-day, and was forced to supply this defect by a particular contrivance of my own, which I think needless to mention here : that deficiency being soon made up by the needful materials I found afterwards in the captain's, gunner's, and carpenter's chests and parcels, where I got not only pen and ink, but likewise sea compasses, and other mathematical instruments ; and, above all the rest, three English Bibles, with several other good English books which I carefully laid up, in order to make use of them at proper intervals. But notwithstanding I was thus plentifully supplied, I still wanted several other necessaries ; as needles and thread, and more particularly a pick-axe and shovel for removing the earth, &c.

It was a full year before I had finished my little fortification ; and after I had done that in the best manner the nature of the place and my circumstances would allow, I began to grow e.

tle more familiar with my solitude, and to consider the best methods possible to render my desolate state as easy as I could ; and, here it was that I began the following Journal.

J O U R N A L.

September 30th, 1656

I Was forced by shipwreck upon this desolate island, which I called the Island of Despair ; next day I spent in reflecting upon the miserableness of my condition, which represented to me nothing but death, and the worst of death too, viz. either to be starved for want of victuals, or to be devoured by wild beasts.

October 1st, To my great comfort, I discovered the ship drove to the shore, from whence I had some hopes, that when the storm was abated, I might recover something towards my present subsistence, especially considering I observed the ship lie, in a great measure, upright, and one side of her perfectly dry, upon which I fell immediately to wading over the sands, and with great difficulty and danger I got on board.

To the 14th of this month I spent in making voyages backwards and forwerds, to and from the ship, the weather being all the while wet and uncertain.

Oct. 20. My raft with my goods was overset, most of which, however, I recovered at low water.

Oct. 25. It blew a sort of storm, & rained hard, so that the ship was dashed to pieces, and nothing of her was to be seen but the very hulk at low water: and this day I thought it proper to secure the effects I had preserved from the weather.

Oct 26 I wandered about to try if I could find a place proper to fix my abode : and accordingly, towards the evening, I found out a rock, where I might erect a wall, and fortify myself.

November 1st, I placed my tent by the side of a rock, and took up my lodging in a hammock, very contentedly for that night.

Nov. 2. I made a fence about my tent with timber, chests and boards.

Nov. 3. I shot two wild fowls, which

proved very good meat; and in the afternoon I made me a fort of a table.

Nov. 4. I began to live regularly. In the morning I walked out for an hour or two, and afterwards worked till about two, then eat my dinner of fuch provifions as I had: after dinner I commonly flept an hour or two: and the wheather being extreme hot, I could not go to work till towards the evening.

Nov. 5. I went out with my gun, & the dog I had brought out of the fhip; I fhot a wild cat, but her flefh was good for nothing, only I preferved her fkin: I faw a great flock of wild birds; and was wonderfully terrified at the fight of fome monftrous feals which I faw on the fand; but as foon as they faw me, they made off to the fea.

Nov. 9. I finifhed my table. From the 7th to the 12th, the weather being fair, I worked very hard, only I refted upon the 11th; which according to my computation, I took to be Sunday.

Nov. 12. The weather was very wet and formy, with thunder and lightning.

On the 14th, I made provision to secure my powder, which I perfected on
the 15th and 16th; and the 17th I began to dig upon the rock, but was prevented for want of proper implements;
and, on the 18th I found a tree, the
wood of which was very hard, and out
of that, with the greatest difficulty, I
made a sort of a spade; in doing it, I
almost spoiled my axe which might have
been of ill consequence.

Nov. 23d, When I had got my tools
into the best order I could, I spent all
my time to the 10th of December in fini-
shing my cave, and lay in my tent e-
very night unless the weather was so wet
that I could not lye dry: and withal,
had so well thatched it over with flags,
the leaves of the trees, &c. that I thought
myself tolarable secure.

Dec. 10th. I had no sooner finished
my habitation, but a great part of the
roof fell in upon me; and it was a
great mercy I had not perished in my
ruins: and indeed it gave me a great
deal of trouble before I could repair
it effectually; and after I had done

what I could, I spent several days in putting my things in proper order, and had variety of weather to the same.

Dec. 27th, In my rounds, I chanced to meet some goats; shot one of them, and lamed another, which I led home, bound up its leg, and in a very little time it grew well, and was so tame and familiar, that it followed me every were like a dog, which put the notion in my head, to bring up this wild creature, as often as I could take them alive, that I might have a stock to subsist upon, in case I should live after my powder was exhausted.

Dec. 28th, 29th, 30th, The weather was so very hot, that I was forced to keep within my shelter.

Janu. 1st, Tho' the weather continued very sulty, yet necessity compelled me to go abroad with my gun. In the vallies I found great number of goats, but they were so very shy, I could by no means come at one of them.

From Janu. 3d to the 4th my business was to search the island and to finish my wall. In search I found great number of fowl, much like our Englifh pigeons ; I fhot one of them, which proved excellent food : and now it was a very providential thing happened, which was thus.

Whilft I was rummaging among my movables, what would fall in my hands but a bag, which, I fuppofe, might be of ufe to hold corn for the fowls in the fhip. I fuppofed to make ufe of it to hold fome of my powder, and fo fhook out the duft and loofe corn upon the fide of the rock, not in the leaft fufpecting the confequence. The rain had fallen in a great quantity a few days before ; a month after, to my great furprize, I difcovered fomething fpring up very green and flourifhing, and as I came daily to view it, I faw feveral ears of green barley, of the very fame fize and fhape of thofe in England.

My thoughts was very much confufed at the unexpected fight ; and I muft own I had the vanity to imagine, that providence had ordered this on purpofe for my fubfiftence. Great was my acknowledgments, and thankfulnefs to

almighty God, for his mercies to me
in this defolate place; which were in-
finitely heightened, when at the fame
time, I obſerved ſome rice ſtalks wonderfully green and flouriſhing, which
made me conclude, there muſt conſequently be more corn in the iſland; and
accordingly, I ſpent ſeveral days in
ſearching the rocks; when, at length,
it came into my mind, that I had ſhaken
the bag in the very ſpot where theſe
blades of corn were growing.

It was about the latter end of June
before theſe ears of corn grew ripe,
and then I laid them up exceeding carefully, expecting I ſhould, one day, reap
the advantage of this little crop, which
I uſed all my induſtry to improve; and
yet it was four years before I could eat
any barley bread, and much longer before I had any benefit from my rice.
After this, with indefatigable care and
induſtry, I finiſhed my wall, ordering
it ſo, that I had no way to go into my
fortreſs but by a ladder.

April 16th, I finiſhed my ladder, and
and went up and pulled it after me, as

I always did, and in truth had so well fortified myself, that I was, as I thought indifferent well secured against any surprize: nevertheless, as I was one day sitting in my cave, there happened such a sudden earthquake, that the roof of my little fortress, that I had finished with so much labour, came tumbling down upon my head; upon which, with the greatest amazement, I ran to my ladder, and got out of my cave, and saw the top of a vast rock roll into the sea, and expected every moment the whole island would be swallowed up.

In this fright I remained for some moments, till I perceived the fury of the motion began to abate; but it was not long before I was under new apprehensions on account of a violent tempest that attended. This dreadful storm continued for about three hours, and then followed such a heavy rain, that my tent was quite overflowed: upon which I concluded my habitation was ill situated, and determined as soon as possible, to build me one in a more convenient place.

April 29th, 30th, Were spent in con-contriving how, and in what manner, I should fix my new abode; and herein I was under the greatest concern, having no tools fitting for such an undertaking: however, I spent several days in whetting and grinding my tools.

May 1. As I was walking along the sea-side, I found a barrel of gun powder, and divers other pieces of the ship, which the violence of the storm had thrown on the sand. I saw also the remaining part of the ship thrown up by the tempest very near the shore, and resolved to get to her as soon as I could but at that time found it impracticable.

I continued to work upon the wreck till the 24th, and every day recovered something that would be of use to me, and got together so many planks, and so much iron, lead, and other necessaries, that if I had tools, and skill, I might have built me a boat, which I wanted extremley.

June 16. As I was strolling towards the sea, I found a large turtle: the 17th I spent in cooking it: I found in

her threescore and ten eggs, and the
flesh was the most delicious meat that
ever I tasted.   The 18th I staid within
the whole day, there being a continu-
al rain, with storms of wind and lightning.

From the 19th to the 27th of June
I was very sick, and had got a terrible
ague, which often held me for nine or
ten hours with extreme violence. --
Upon the 28th I began to recover a little, but was very restless in the night,
and was worse : as often as I laid my
eyes together, I was tormented with
hideous dreams, and dreadful aparitl-
ons : it is impossible for me to express
the agonies I was under by these repeated admonitions, as I took them to be ;
my father's advice and reproof came
into my mind whether I would or not,
and shocked me exceedingly, & would
often make me reflect, that the justice
of God followed me, and severe punish-
ment was justly owing to my disobedi-
ence and wicked life.

June 28. I slept pretty well most
part of the night, which refreshed me

very much ; in the morning I eat a
biſcuit, and drank ſome waters-mixed
with rum ; I boiled a piece of goat's
fleſh for my dinner, but eat very little,
and at night I ſupped upon three of my
turtle's eggs : after ſupper I attempted
to walk out with my gun, but found
myſelf too weak, and ſo returned to
my habitation.

Here conſcience flew in my face,
reprehended me as a blaſphemer, and
a reprobate, for ſaying in my agonies,
" What have I done to be diſtinguſhed
in all this ſcene of miſery ?" Methought
I heard a voice anſwering me, " Un-
grateful wretch ! dare you aſk what
you have done ? Look upon your paſt
life, and then aſk thyſelf; why thou was
not drowned in Yarmouth Roads, or
killed by the Sallee rovers ? why not devoured by wild beaſt in the deſarts of
Africa, or drowned here with the reſt
of my companions ?"

Struck dumb by theſe ſevere reflections, and fearing the return of my
ague, I began at length to conſider
what was beſt to be done, to free my

felf from this diftemper; and having heard that the Caftilians ufed tobacco for moft of their difeafes, I was refolved to try this experiment.

I tried feveral ways with the tobacco; firft took a leaf and chewed it, which made me very fick and almoft ftupified me: next I fteeped it in rum, refolving to take a **good** dofe of it when I went to bed; and then I put fome into a pan and burnt it, holding my nofe over the fmoke as long as I could endure without fuffocation. After thefe feveral operations I fell into a fweat, and flept quietly and well for thirteen or fourteen hours; and when I got up in the morning, I found my fpirits revived, my ftomach much better, and I grew exceeding hungry, which I had not been for fome time paft; in fhort I miffed my fit the next time, and found that I every day grew ftronger and better.

The 30th, I ventured out with my gun, and killed a fowl not much unlike a brand goofe, but did not eat of the flefh, chufing rather to dine upon two or three more of my turtle's eggs. In the evening I renewed my medicine, notwithstanding which, I had a little spice of my fit the next day : and therefore, on the 2d of July, I took my medicine as at first : and on the 4th, which was the day in which I expected the return of my fit, the ague left me, which was no small joy to me ; and indeed the goodness of God, on this occasion, affected me so sensibly, that I fell on my knees, and returned thanks in the most devout and solemn manner.

July 4. I walked out with my gun, but my distemper had reduced me so low, I could go but a little way at a time ; for the experiment having weakened me exceedingly, I was not able to walk but a short way at once. I had now been in the island about ten months, and all the while had not seen either man or woman ; and so growing better, I began to think myself sole monarch of the isle ; and growing indifferently well, resolved to take a tour round the island, in order to view the extent of my dominions, and to make what difcoveries I could.

The 15th I began my journey; and among other things, I found a little brook of running water, on the bank, of which were feveral pleafant meadows covered with grafs; and among other things, I faw feveral ftalks of tobacco, and other plants I knew nothing of; among the reft, I found fome fugar canes, feveral plants of aloe wands, with thefe difcoveries I returned well fatisfied to my little caftle, and flept that night very comfortably.

The next day going the fame way, and further than before, I found a country full of wood, and extremely delightful. The melons lay upon the ground in great quantities, and large clufters of grapes hung among the trees and though I was mighty glad of this difcovery, yet I eat very fparingly of them, for fear of putting myfelf in a flux or a fever.

The night coming on, I climbed up into a tree and having fixed myfelf as fecure as poffible, flept very comfortably, though it was the firft time I had

er lain out of my habitation : when
e morning came I proceeded, with
e greateſt pleaſure about four miles
rther, and at the end of this valley
found a ſpring of excellent water,
d the country all around the moſt
eautiful I ever ſaw : and now I was
ſolved to lay up as much of the fruit
 poſſible.

July 21. Having prepared two bags,
returned thither again, in order to
ing home to my caſtle as much of the
veral ſorts of fruits as I could, that
night have a ſtock by me againſt I
ould want it ; and now I began to
lect that this part of the iſland was
initely the beſt to inhabit in ; but
en I thought, at the ſame time, that
r moved from my preſent place of
ode, I ſhould loſe the proſpect of
 ſea ; and ſo if providence ſhould
ler a ſhip on that coaſt, I ſhould
e all poſſibility of deliverance : how-
er, the place was ſo delightful, I
s reſolved to build me a ſort of a
t of a country ſeat there, which took
the remainder of the month of July.

'Here it was I dried my grapes which I afterwards carried to my old habitation, for a winter supply. Upon the 14th day of August, the rain began to fall with great violence, which made me judge it proper to retire to my castle for shelter. The rains continued to fall more or less to the middle of October, and sometimes with that violence, that for several days I could not stir out of my cave, till I was constrained to it by the pure want of food. I went out twice; the first time I shot a goat and the second I found a turtle as large as the former.

Sep. 30. Casting up the notches on the post, I found they amounted exactly to 365: I concluded this to be the annual of my landing. And after I had returned thanks for my wonderful preservation in this desolate island, I went to my bed and slept very contentedly.

Before I proceed further in my journal, I must take the liberty to put the reader in mind of the barley and the rice: I had saved about thirty stalk

of the former, and twenty of the latter ; and concluding the feafon to be
proper, I dug up fome ground with my
wooden fpade, and fowed it, which at
the proper time grew up, and anfwered my expectations.

The wet weather was no fooner
gone, but my inclination lead me to the
bower I had built on the other fide of
the ifland, which I found whole and entire as I had left it and the ftakes all
growing, much after nature of our wil-
lows, which in time made a noble fence
as I fhall have occafion to fpeak of
more particularly hereafter.

And now I conceived that the fea-
fons of the year was divided into wet
and dry, and not into fummer and
winter as in Europe.

And as the winds continued to blow
the wet feafon would continue longer
or fhorter ; and after I had made thefe
and the like obfervations I always took
care to provide neceffaries, that I
might ftay within during the wetnefs
of the weather, and in that time I took
care to make fuch tools as I moft want-

ed.

The firſt thing I attempted, was to make a baſket, which after much labor and difficulty, I effected ; but the two things I moſt wanted were entirely out of my power, viz. ſome caſks to hold my liquors, and ſmall pots to boil and ſtew my meat, and alſo a tobacco pipe, for which I at laſt found out a remedy.

After the weather grew fair, my reſolution of further viewing the whole iſland took place ; and accordingly, taking my dog and gun, and other neceſſaries proper, I ſet forward, and having paſſed the vale where the bower ſtood, I came in ſight of the ſea, lying to the W. and when it was a clear day, I could diſcover land, but could not tell whether it was an iſland, or the continent ; neither could I tell what place this might be ; only I thought it was America, and conſequently that part of the country that lies between the Spaniſh territories and the Braſils, which abounds with cannibals who devour human kind.

In viewing this part of the iſland, I found it was much more pleaſant and fruitful than where I had pitched my tent. Here were great numbers of parrots, and with great difficulty I got one of them, which I carried home with me, but it was a great while before I could tame it and bring it to ſpeak, even ſo much as to call me by my name.

In the low grounds I found great numbers of hares and foxes, and abundance of fowls of different kinds, with great quantities of grapes and other excellent fruit. In this expedition I did not travel above two miles a day, being deſirous to make what diſcoveries I could ; and when I came to the ſea ſhore, I was amazed to ſee it ſo exceedingly beautiful, and ſo full of excellent fiſh ; but tho this journey I muſt confeſs was very delightful to me, yet ſtill my ſecret inclination led me to my old habitation : ſo that after I had ſet up a ſort of a land mark for my guide in future, I koncluded to return back

D

by a different way than that I came; and as I was making the beſt of my way, my dog happened to ſurpriſe a kid, which I reſcued from him, and led home in order to try if I could raiſe a breed, which I was ſatisfied would be of ſome uſe to me.

After I had been about a month on this expedition, I returned to my little caſtle, and repoſed myſelf with great pleaſure in my hammock, and indeed continued a week within, to reſt and refreſh myſelf; and now I began to think of the kid I had left behind me in the bower, and reſolved immediately to fetch it home. When I came there I found it almoſt ſtarved, I gave it ſome meat, poor creature, and in gratitude for its deliverance, it followed me, as naturally as my dog, quite home to my caſtle, which afterwards kept as one of my domeſtics.

The wet ſeaſon being come, I kept myſelf within; and, upon the 30th of of September, it being the third year of my abode on the iſland, I paid my ſolemn acknowledgments to Almighty

God for my prefervation, and entered myfelf with a world of reflections upon my prefent and former condition. And as I was one morning fadly poundering on my prefent ftate, I happened to open my Bible, when the following words immediately occured, I will never leave thee, nor forfake thee, which I prefently took as directed to myfelf, and muft own the expreffion gave me a great deal of fecret fatisfaction.

The beginning of this year I fixed my daily employments as follow; the morning I fpent my devotions, and paying my duty to God ; after I had done that, I went out with my gun to feek provifions : which after I had got, took up fome time in dreffing and cooking. In the middle of the day, I was forced to lye by, by reafon of the exclufive heats, and the reft of the time I fpent in making and contriving fuch neceffaries as I ftood moft in need of.

But now the time of my little harveft coming on I had the defired profpect of a good crop, but my hopes were fadly difappointed by the goats

and hares. who have tafted the fweet-
nefs of my corn, had cropped it fo clofe,
that it had not ftrength to fhoot up into a ftock ; to prevent this I was forced to make an hedge round it ; but I
had no fooner done this, but I was in-
fefted with vermin of another fpecies.
My back was no fooner turned, but
whole flocks of birds came and deftroyed what the others had left ; I let fly
upon thefe, and killed three of them,
which I hung up as a terror to the reft,
upon ftakes, that they not only forfook
the corn, but that part of the ifland for
ever afterwards.

My corn growing ripe, and harveft
coming on, I cut it down and carried
home the ears; and after I had rubbed
them- and thrafhed them in the beft
manner I could, I conjectured the pro-
duce of the barley was about two bufh-
els and a half, and that of the rice
much about the fame quantity.—— And
now I plainly faw, by the providence
of God, I fhould be fupplied with corn,
though at the fame time, I wanted all
manner of neceffaries for making in in-

to bread, which, with the greateſt labour and difficulty, I afterwards ſupplied.

My feed being thus increaſed, my
next care was to prepare more land to
fow in; and accordingly, I fixed upon
two large plats upon the back fide of my
caſtle, which I prepared with great
pains, and put it into the ground, and
after made a hedge round it, to defend
it from vermin.

In ſhort, my corn increaſed to that
degree, that I thought I might now
venture to eat fome of it; but how to
make it into bread, was ſtill the difficulty; and yet even this found means
to furmount at laft, and fo as in all o-
ther emergencies, I found a remedy
beyond my expectation.

After I had procured every thing
needful for making my bread, which
you may imagine was no fmall fatisfaction, the profpect of land which I had
feen on the other fide of the water
came afreſh into my mind ; but how I
ſhould come at it I was utterly at a lofs.
I tried to recover the ſhip's boat, and

then to make a canoe, but all in vain; and here I could not forbear reflecting upon the folly of those that undertake matters they are not able to go through with.

I was in the midst of my projects, when my fourth year expired since I had been cast on the island; nor did I forget to keep my anniversary with that solemnity and devotion as I had done the year before: I began to think myself seperated from the world, and from all opportunities of human conversation: I now had nothing to covet, being, as it were, an emperor, or king of a whole country, where I had nobody to controul me, nor nobody to govern but myself.

These thoughts made me look upon the things of this world with a sort of a religious contempt, and rendered me easy in my desolate and melancholy condition; for having made God's mercies to me matters of the highest consolation, I relinquished all pensive thoughts, and dismal apprehensions, and reſigned myſelf up entirely to Gods providence.

My ink was quite gone, and my biſcuit almoſt exhauſted ; my linen was worn out, only ſome of the ſailors chequer'd ſhirts remained, which were of mighty uſe to me in the hot weather. My cloaths and hat were quite worn, but thoſe I ſupplied by the help of my goat ſkin, of which I firſt made a ſort of cap, and then a waiſtcoat, and open knee'd breeches, with the hair on the outſide : and thus being perfectly at eaſe in my mind, I ſpent my time in contemplating the mercies of heaven, and was raviſhed to think that at one time or other I ſhould be delivered from my preſent misfortunes, and placed out of the reach of them for ever.

For five years after this, nothing worth mentioning happened, only at ſpare times, I had finiſhed a ſmall canoe, with which, at all hazards, I reſolved to try to diſcover the circumference of my dominions ; and in order to it, I put proviſions on board, wit

ammunition, and all other neccefaries
fit for the expedition.

It was on the 16th of November, in
the 9th year of my reign, that I began
this voyage; which was much longer
than I expected, by reafon I had many
difficulties to encounter I did not fuf-
pect; and, indeed, the rocks were fo
high, and ran fo far into the fea, that
I often refolved to turn back, rather
than run the rifk of being driven fo far
out to fea that I could by no means get
back again.

In this confufion, I came to anchor as
near to the fhore as poffible : to which
I waded, and clambering up to the top
of an high hill, I viewed the extent of
my dominions, and at all hazards refolved to purfue my voyage. It is endlefs
to relate what dangers my rafhnefs ex-
pofed me to : I was driven by the current fo far into the fea, that I had hardly any profpect to get back again ; not
by all I could do with my paddles, which
I had made to fupply the place of fculls
to help me ; and now I had no profpect
but perifhing in the fea, when my pro-

vifions were fpent, or, if a ftorm fhould arife, before. However, by the lucky change of the wind, or rather, by the particular providence of God, I was driven back again to the ifland, and, to my unfpeakable joy, I came to fhore where, being exceedingly fatigued with watching and hard labour, I laid me down and took a little repofe. After I awaked and had dreffed myfelf as u-fual, I laid up my boat in a fmall con-venient creek fit for that purpofe, and taking my gun, &c. I made the beft of my way towards my bower, and again I laid me down to reft, but it was not long before I was greatly furprized & frightened with a voice, which called, " Robin Crufoe, poor Robin Crufoe, where have you been, poor Robin Cru-foe!" Upon which I ftarted up in a great confufion; and cafting my eyes around I faw my parrot fitting upon the hedge, and then I knew it was fhe that called to me, but was ftrangely furprized how the creature could come there, and why it fhould fix upon that place above the reft: the bird came to me as foon as I called it, and it perched on my thumb as usual, and seemed to signify a great deal of joy for my return.

This voyage had cured me of a great deal of my rambling inclination; insomuch that I began to lay aside all hopes of deliverance; so I led a retired life, and in a very contented manner passed away near twelve months, spending my time in making instruments, and doing such things as I found were absolutely necessary. both for my present and future subsistence.

My next consideration was, my powder growing short, what I should do to kill the goats and fowl to live upon. I had abundance of contrivances in my head to try to catch the goats alive, particularly the she goats with young; and at length I found my desire : for making pitfalls, and bating them with some of my corn, one morning I found in one of them an old he goat, and in the other three young ones, viz. a male and two fe-males; the old one was too strong for me, and I could not tell how to master him, but the young ones I

made fhift to get home to my cave;
it was fome time before I could make
them feed, but after they had fome
time been kept without food, I threw
them fome frefh corn, and gave them
fome water, their ftomachs came to
them : and now my next care was to
fecure them fo that they might not run
away : all which, with abundance of
pains and difficulty, I at laft effected,
and withal, by my good ufage of thefe
poor creatures, I had made them fo
tame and familiar, that they would
follow me, and eat my corn out of my
hand : this having anfwered my ends
to all intents and purpofes, I think in
about a year and a halfs time I had got
a good ftock of about twelve, and in
lefs than two years forty three ; and
now I was not only well provided with
goats flefh, but with milk too, which
was another blefling I had little reafon
to expect.

Being thus happy, and having almoft
forgot all hopes of liberty, I lived as
well as the nature of my condition could
poffibly allow ; and indeed, it was a

very diverting fight to fee me fet in
ftate at my dinner, all alone by myfelf,
like a king; and it would have been a
very pleafant object to have feen me
in my goat fkin drefs, and other habili-
ments.

My chief concern was now about
my coat, which I was extremely unwilling to lofe, having coft me fo much
hard labour. I went by land to the
place where I left it, but found there
was no way to bring it off, without
running the fame rifk I was lately expo-
fed to, which I thought too dangerous
for a fecond experiment; and therefore I refolved upon another expedient
which was to make another canoe, and
leave it on the other fide of the ifland.

And here I think it may not be im-
proper to inform the reader, that I had
two plantations in the ifland: the firft
was my little fort or caftle, where I
had made feveral improvements; and
my fecond was my bower, or country
feat. where my grapes, and the encle-
fures for my goates and feveral other.

conveniencies, made it a very pleaſant and agreeable retirement.

From this place it was that I uſed to go often to view my boat; and now I ſhall relate a thing that gave me the moſt diſquiet of any thing I had ever met with, ſince my firſt coming into the iſland.

It may be well ſuppoſed, that after I had been ſo long in this deſolate part of the world, nothing could have been more ſurprizing than to have ſeen any human creature; but one day, as I was going to my boat as uſual, I perceived on the ſand the print of a mans naked foot, and had I ſeen an apparition, I could not have been more terrified. I looked round me on all ſides, but could not hear or ſee any thing: I obſerved the tramplings, and was convinced, from all the ſigns, that ſome foot had been there, and in the deepeſt confuſion, I returned back to my habitation.

That night I never cloſed my eyes, and was full of the moſt diſmal apprehenſions that I was ever in, in all my

E

life. Sometimes I had the vanity to think it muft be the devil : at other times I thought it rather fome favage, that the current had driven in, and not liking the place, was fecretly gone off to fea again. Happy was I in the thought that none of the favages had feen me, and yet, at the fame time I was exceedingly terrified left they fhould have feen my boat, and fo come in great numbers, and find me out, & devour me and all my little ftock, that I had been fo long a gathering. Thefe thoughts afflicted me extremely, and yet, after mature confideration, I concluded it was my beft way to throw myfelf upon the fovereign Governor of the world, and to fubmit entirely to his mercy and providence.

After a world of fears and apprehenfions, for three nights and days. I ventured out of my fortrefs, I milked my goats, and after I had put every thing in order, not without the greateft confternation, I went again to the fhore to make my further obfervations, and upon the whole, concluded, that either the island was inhabited, or that some persons had been on shore, and that I might be surprised before I was aware. This put several frightful notions into my head, insomuch, that sleep was an entire stranger to me; my whole thot's being taken up in nothing but my preservation. I put my little castle in the best posture of defence I was able, and placed all my guns so that they might be serviceable, if I should have occasion to make use of them.

I divided my goats into several parcels; ten she goats, and two he ones I put into one place of the island, and the other ten with two he ones, in another; and whilst I was in search of this latter, which was on the western part of this island, I thought I discovered a boat, but at too great a distance to make what she was. Being come to the shore upon the S. W. part of the island, I was convinced they were savages, seeing the place covered over with the sculls and mangled limbs of human bodies, I observed likewise a sort of circle in the midst; I could perceive there had been a fire, about which, I conjectured, these wretches fat, and unnaturally facraficed and devoured their fellow creatures.

The horror and loathfulnefs of this dreadful fpectacle confounded me fo, that though I was fatisfied thefe favages never came to that part of the ifland & where I was, yet fuch an abhorrance of them had feized me, that for two years I confined myfelf to my caftle, my country feat, and my enclofures and thus my circumftances remained for fome time undifturbed. But ftill my grand intention remained ; which was to try if I could deftroy fome of thofe favages and fave a victim that I might afterwards make my fervant.

Many were my projects and contrivances to bring this about, at length I came to this refolution, to lye privately in ambufh in fome convenient place, and let fly upon them with my guns firft, and then with my piftols and fword in hand ; and fo much did this propofal pleafe my fancy, that I was fully refolved to put it in practice the firft oppertunity; and accordingly, I found a place convenient for my purpoſe : but at the ſame time, had ſeveral checks of conſcience, and reaſonings with myſelf concerning the lawfulneſs and juſtice of the attempt, and after a long debate, I concluded to lay aſide the deſign.

Whilſt I was cutting down the wood one day, to make charcoal to dreſs my meat, and do the family neceſſaries, I perceieed a very large cavity, and going towards it, I could perceive two large eyes ſtaring upon me; upon which I made haſte out, extremely terrified, not imagining what it could be that looked ſo frightfully ; however, after I recovered from my ſurpriſe, I went in again, reſolving at all hazards, to ſee what it was, and when I came near enough to diſcern it perfectly what ſhould it be after all, but a monſtrous he goat, lying on the ground and gaſping for life, and dying for mere old age.

The creature was unable to ſtand, ſo I let him lye, and employed myſelf in viewing the place, I obſerved a ſort of entrance but so low, that I muft be forced to creep into it upon my hands & knees: I had no candle, and the place was dark, and so I fufpended my enterprife till the next day, when I returned with fix large ones of my own making.

After I had paffed the ftrait paffage, I found the roof rofe higher up & fure when I came further in, no mortal ever faw a more beautiful fight, the walls and the roof reflected a thoufand lights from my two candles ; and indeed it feemed to be the moft delightful grotto I had ever heard of. In fhort, I could find no fault but in the entrance, and that I thought to render more proper for my defence and fecurity, and therefore I determined to make this place my principal magazine, and accordingly, I brought hither, fome arms & ammunition, judging it impoffible for me to be furprifed by the favages in that faftnefs.

I think I was now in the 23d year of my reign, & tolarably eafy in my condition. By this time my parret had learned to talk Englifh very well, and many diverting hours we uſed to have together, my dog died of old age, and my cats increaſed & multiplied ſo faſt; that I was often forced to deſtroy ſome of them, leſt I ſhould be over run by their numbers, I always kept two or three domeſtic goats about me, and had ſeveral fowls that built and bred about my caſtle, ſo that I wanted nothing but an honeſt companion or two to make me as happy as I could wiſh : but alas ! what unforeſeen events deſtroy the uncertain enjoyments of human happineſs.

It was now December the time of my harveſt, when going out one morning early, there appeared to me from the ſhore, about two miles diſtance from me, a flaming light from that part of the iſland where I before had obſerved ſome ſavages had been on my ſide of the water.

Terrified with this unuſual ſpectacle, and being under diſmal apprehenſions, that theſe ſavages would find me out, and deſtroy me, I went directly home to my caſtle, and ſhut myſelf up as

faſt as I could, and put myſelf into a
poſture of defence ; and after this I
got up to the top of the rock, and
viewing with my proſpect glaſs, I could
diſcern no leſs than 9 naked ſavages
ſitting round a fire, and eating as I
ſuppoſed, human fleſh, with their two
canoes hauled upon the ſhore, waiting
for the tide carrying them back a-
gain.

Nothing could expreſs my deteſtation of ſo horrid a ſight, eſpecially
when I found they were gone and I had
been at the place of ſacrifice, and ſaw
the limbs and fleſh of human creatures
lye torn and mangled upon the ground:
in ſhort, my indignation againſt them
roſe ſo high, that, let the conſequence
be what it would, I was determined to
be revenged upon them the firſt time
they ſhould come thither, though I
ſhould loſe my life in the attempt. I
found afterwards that they did not
come over to this iſland very often,
and, as near as I can remember, it was
a year or more before I ſaw any more
of them. But before I proceed farther,

I have another account that will deserve the reader's attention.

It was on the 16th of May, according to my wooden calender, after a very terrible storm, when I was alarmed with the noise of a gun, as fired from a ship in distress, when with my glass, I went up to the rock, where I had not been a moment, but a flame of fire gave notice of another gun, and then I was confirmed in my opinion, that it could be nothing else but a ship in distress; which with my glass, soon discovered to be true, and that the wreck was upon these hidden rocks, where I was in great danger of being lost in my boat.

I made a fire upon the hill by way of signal, and they saw it, and answered it with several guns. The weather was very hazy, and so I could not at that time discover either at what distance the ship lay, or what she was; but the weather clearing up, I saw a ship cast away at some distance at sea.

I had several notions concerning

them, as it is natural in such cases,
but considering seriously the place
where they were, and all other circumstances, I could not conceive any
possibility but that they must be lost ;
and indeed, to the last year of my being on this island, I never knew of any
that were saved out of this ship, I only
saw the body of a boy that was drove
on shore, but I could not discover by
him of what nation they were.

The sea was now very calm which
tempted me to venture to the wreck,
not only in hopes to get something I
wanted, but likewise, if there were a-
ny body left alive in the ship to endeavour to save their lives. This resolution so far prevailed, that I went home
immediately, and got every thing ready for the voyage; and accordingly,
after a great deal of labour, hazard &
difficulty, I at length got to the wreck,
which I beheld with the greatest pity &
concern. By her building, I found she
was a Spaniard, and had endured a
terrible conflict before she was lost.

When I was come near to her, I saw

a dog on board, who no fooner faw me
but he feil a yelping and howling, and
I no fooner called to him, but the poor
creature jumped into the fea, & fwam
to me, and I took him into the boat
almoft famifhed. When I came into the
fhip, the firft thing I beheld was two
drowned men in the arms of each other,
I found fhe was a rich fhip, & as I had
reafon to believe bound home from the
Spanifh Weft Indies. What became of
the reft of the failors I could not tell,
there being none of their bodies on
board befides the two already mentioned.

As I was rummaging about her, I
found feveral things I wanted, viz. a
fire fhovel and tongs, two brafs kettles,
a pot to make chocolate, fome horns
of fine glazed powder, and gridiron, &
feveral other neceffaries. Thefe I put
on board my boat, together with two
chefts, and a cafk of rum ; and after a
great deal of toil & difficulty, got back
fafe to the ifland.

I repofed myfelf that night in the
boat, and the next day landed my car-

go, which I carried to my grotto, and having examined my effects, I found in the two chests several things that I wanted, particularly some shirts and hankerchiefs, 3 bags of pieces of eight, all which I would willingl have given for five or six pair of English shoes and stockings.

After I had stowed all this new cargo in my cave I made the best of my way to my castle, where I found every thing as I left it, so that I had nothing to do but to take care of my domesticks and now wanting nothing that was requisite, for the support of life, I might have lived very quit, had not my constant apprehension of the savages disturbed me, on which account I seldom went far abroad, if I did, it was to the eastern part of the island, where I very well knew they never came, and for two years, I lived in this anxious condition, my head being always full of projects, how I might get away from this desolate place.

I observed before, though I was tolerable secure against the reach of want, and had all the diversion the nature of the island would allow; yet the thoughts of my deliverance were still uppermost, as my reader will easily perceive by the following relation, in which I shall give a short account of the schemes and projects I had for my escape.

As I lay on my bed one night in March the 24th year of my solitude, I ran thro' all the accidents of my life, from my first remembrance to the present time, & found all along that the providence of God had been exceeding kind and munificent to me: and when I considered more particularly, how many dangers I had passed, it could not but make me devoutly thankful to my great deliverer, without whose assistance I must have perished inevitably.

After I had thus briefly debated with myself my present and former condition, I began next to consider the nature of these savages, & the country where they inhabited, how far it was to the place from whence they came, & what boats they have to bring them over his ther; and at the same time had some notions to go over to their side to see what discoveries I could make.

I had no notions, that if by any method I could get upon the continent, I might in time meet with a ship to carry me to Europe, for here I looked upon myself to be the most miserable man living, and prefered even death itself to my stay in this desolate island. Whilst my thoughts were thus in confusion, I had no notion of any thing but my voyage to the continent; & indeed so much was I inflamed with these new notions, that I, in a great measure, forgot my duty to God and was almost to a state of desperation; & after many thot's and strugglings in my mind I came at length, to this conclusion, viz. that the only probable way to escape, was to get one of these savages, which I could find no other way to bring about, than by venturing my life to deliver him out of the jaws of these devourers: which I thought must inspire him with gratitude to his preser-
ver.

These were my first resolutions; but I think it was at least a year and a half before I could find an opportunity of putting them in execution. To the best of my remembrance, it was the third day of April, early in the morning, when I was surprized with the sight of five canoes all upon the shore together, on my side of the island, and the creatures that belonged to them, all landed, and out of sight.

At first, I thought all these boats must bring too many to be attacked by a single person, and was in a mighty confusion what was best to be done: however, being impatient to see something of their management, I took my gun, and went secretly to the top of the hill, where by the help of my perspective glass, I observed no less than 30 sitting round a fire, and feasting upon what meat they had dressed; what it was I could not distinguish: but they were all dancing around the flames, using many frightful and barbarous gestures.

Whilst I was looking earnestly on

these wretches, I could discern them dragging two miserable creatures out of one of the boats. It was not long before I saw one of them knocked down and three or four of them fell to cutting and mangling his body, in order to devour him

Whilst the other miserable creature stood expecting every moment the fate of his companion; inspired with the hopes of life, he gave a sudden start from them and ran with great swiftness towards my castle, where I was apprehensive he would fly for protection. I was glad to see he had the heels of them, and from his swiftness concluded would presently lose sight of them, and save his life. There was a little creek just before them where I was afraid the poor victim would be taken, if he could not swim, but it happened that he swam very well, and soon got over, and ran again with his former swiftness. Two swam over after him, but the other that could not swim, returned back to his companions. And

now or never, I thought, was my time
to procure a savage for my companion.
Accordingly, I came down from the
rock, took up my two guns, resolving

to save the victim if possible; and in
order to it came a nearer way, & put
myself between the pursuers and the
pursued, beckoning to the latter to

stand still, who you must imagine, was
not a little amazed at the sight of me.
The first pursuer I knocked down with
the stock of my piece, and the other
who I perceived was preparing his bow
and arrow to shoot me, I let fly at him,
& killed him dead upon the spot. The
poor frighted Indian was terribly amazed to see the fire, and hear the noise
of the gun : however, I made signs to
him to come to me, which at length he
did, but not without a great deal of
fear & trembling, being afraid I should
kill him too. I did all I could to con-
vince him of his mistake, and at length
so far convinced him by the signs I made
him, that he came to me' and threw
himself at my feet, and took one of my
feet, and put upon his head, which was
a token it seems, of his resolution he
would be my slave for ever : upon which
I took him up, made much of him, &
encouraged him in the best manner I
could,

By this time I saw the savage I had
knocked down began to recover, which
made my slave as much afraid as before

but I ſoon prevented his fright, by pre-
ſenting my piece at him ; but my ſavage oppoſed my ſhooting him, making
a ſign to lend him my ſword which
hung by my ſide ; and no ſooner had
I granted his requeſt but away he run
to his enemy, and very dexterouſly at
one blow cut of his head, and as a token of triumph, brought it me, together with my ſword, and laid it at my
feet.

The greateſt aſtoniſhment my new
ſervant was in, was, how I came to kill
the ſavage at a diſtance, without a bow
and arrow : and to ſatisfy himſelf in
that matter, he made ſigns to me to
let him go and view the body, which I
granted ; after he had turned him and
viewed the wound the bullet had made
in his breaſt, he took up his bow and
arrows, and came back to me again,
making ſigns to me to give him leave
to bury them, which with my conſent,
he performed with wonderful dexterity. When I perceived he had done,
I called him away, and carried him
directlly to my cave, where I gave him

victuals, and then pointed to him to lye down upon a heap of straw, & take a little reft. He was a very handsome, well proportioned fellow, and in all respects, the moft beautiful Indian I had ever feen. I think he had not flept above an hour, before he came out of the cave to me as I was milking my goats.

Then falling down again, he laid his head flat upon the ground, and fet my other foot upon it, as before, and after this made all poffible figns of thankfulnefs, fubjection, and fubmiffion. I began to fpeak to him, and to teach him to fpeak to me; and firft, I made him know that his name fhould be FRIDAY, which was the day wherein I faved his life, I tought him to fay MASTER, and let him know that was to be my name. The next day I gave him cloaths, at which he feemed pleafed. As we went by the place were he had buried the two men, he pointed exactly to the fpot, making figns that he would dig them up again and eat them; at this I appeared to be very angry, and beck-

oned with my hand to him to come a-
way which he did immediately.

Having now more courage, & confequently more curiofity, I took my
man FRIDAY, with me, giving him the
fword in his hand, with the bow and
arrows at his back, which I found he
could ufe very dexterodfly. I alfo gave
him to carry one gun, and taking two
for myfelf, away we marched to the
place where his enemies had been :
When I came there my blood ran cold
in my veins; the place was covered
with human bones, and the ground dy-
ed with blood : great pieces of flefh
were left here and there, half eaten,
mangled and fcorched. I faw three
fkulls, five hands, and the bones of
three or four legs and feet ; and FRI-
DAY, by his figns, made me underftand
that they brought over four prifoners
to feaft upon, that three of them were
eaten up ; that he, pointing to himfelf, was the fourth : they had been
conquered and taken prifoners in war.

I caufed Friday to collect the re-
mains of this horrid carnage, then to

light a fire, and burn them to ashes.
When this was done we returned to our
castle. The next day I made a little
tent on the outside of my fortification,
and at night took in my ladder, that
he might not be able to get at me
while I slept. But there was no need
of this precaution; for never man had
a more faithful servant; he had the
same affection for me as a child has for
a father, and I dare say, he would
have sacrificed his life to save mine.
I was greatly delighted with him, and
made it my business to teach him every
thing proper to render him useful; especially to speak, and understand me
when I spoke; and he was the aptest
scholar that ever was; then he was so
merry, so diligent, and so pleased
when he could understand me, or make
me understand him, that he was a very
agreeable companion.

After this we returned to my castle,
where I cloathed my man as well as
the nature of the place, and my circumstances would admit. He seemed
at first a little uneasy and aukward in

his new dress; but after he had wore
them four or five days, he grew familiar with them, and seemed extremely
well satisfied. Now, my next concern was, how I might lodge him well
and yet be easy myself; in order to
this, I erected him a little tent between my two fortifications, secured
my arms every night, and made every
thing so safe, that it was impossible for
me to be surprized; though I must
own there was no need of these; for
never man was blessed with a servant
that loved and obeyed him with greater tenderness, fidelity, and affection,
which endeared him to me extremely,
and induced me to think how I might
best acquit myself to him.

I had not been above two or three
days in my castle, when I first proposed to bring him off from his barbarous inclinations to human flesh; in order to which I used several experiments
till the poor creature, who had the
most dutiful and tender regard to every thing I commanded him, was perfectly weaned from his vicious inclina-

tions, and had as deep and fixed abhor-
rence of any such barbarous proceed-
ing as myself: he fell upon his knees,
made all the signs of his aversion he
possibly could, pronouncing many
things I did not understand, only in the
main, I found that his only apprehension was from the fear I should shoot
him ; but the thoughts of the gun, and
the manner of the execution it did
were still in his mind, and he could by
no means be reconciled to it ; he would
not so much as touch it with his finger
for several days, and I believe, if I
had not prevented it, he would have
paid it a sort of adoration. He would
go, as often as my back was turned,
and talk to it in his own dialect ; tho
intent of which, was to desire it not to
kill him.

I had killed a kid, which we brought
home, and the next day I gave him
some of the flesh, both boiled and roast-
ed, with which he was so much delighted, that he gave me signs, which
I perfectly understood, that whilst he
lived, he would never more eat man's

flesh upon any account. And now I began to think it high time to set my servant to work, especially considering I had now two mouths to feed instead of one. I found him extraordinary quick and handy in every thing I set him about, and he had the sense to make me understand that I had more upon my hands upon his account than I had for myself, and that he would spare no pains nor diligence in any thing I should command or direct; and indeed the fellow's honesty and simple integrity grew so conspicuous I realy began to love him entirely; and for his part, I am very well assured there was no love lost. I was desirous to know whether he had a mind to his own country; and having learnt him some English, I asked him several questions, which he answered very pertinently. Particularly I asked him concerning the nature and distance of his country, and their manner of fighting, &c. He had a very good natural genius, and would often answer my questions with

F

very quick and surprizing turns.—
When I spoke about religion, he would
hear me with the greateft reverence
and attention, and would often furprize me with important and unexpected queftions, and in truth, I fpared
no pains to inftruct him according to
the beft of my knowledge. I afked
him, who made him and all the world?
As foon as he underftood what I faid,
he anfwered, God, Benamuckee; but
all that he could fay of him was, "That
he was very old, much older than the
fea and land, the moon and ftars, and
that he lived a great way beyond them
all."

When I had inquired into the manner
of their ferving their God, I proceeded, according to the beft of my knowledge, to inftruct him in the principles
of the Chriftian religion, and laid before him feveral of the chief truths upon which it was grounded; to which
he gave the greateft attention, and
would afk very pertinent queftions, in
order to his information. In fhort, I
foon perceived this poor creature eye-

ry day improved by my inſtruction, and
that my endeavours to inſtruct him
were a great help to myſelf, and
brought thoſe things, freſh into my
memory, which the length of time had
almoſt effaced : ſo that I had the
greateſt reaſon to bleſs providence for
ſending him to me in this ſtate of ſoli-
tude. His company allayed the
thoughts of my miſery, and made my
habitation more comfortable than it
had been ever ſince my firſt coming to
the iſland. It brought into my mind
daily notions of heaven and heavenly
things, and filled me with a ſecret joy
that I was ever brought to this place,
which once I thought the moſt miſera-
ble part of the univerſe.

By this time, Friday began to ſpeak
tolerable Engliſh. We converſed with
great familiarity, and I took a particular pleaſure to relate to him the ſeveral accidents and adventures of my life.
I ſoon made him underſtand the wonderful myſtery, as he conceived it of
the gun powder and ball, and taught
him to ſhoot, which he ſoon learned

to the greateſt perfection I gave him
a knife which he was very proud of ;
likewiſe a belt and a hatchet, which
he hung to his girdle, which, with the
reſt of his accoutrements, made him
look like Don Quixote, when he went
to engage the windmills.   After this
I gave him a particular deſcription of
Europe.   I alſo gave him a large ac-
c unt of my being ſhipwrecked, and
ſhewed him the ruins of the ſhips boat
which tho' it was almoſt rotten and
fallen to pieces, yet I could perceive
he look particular notice of it, which
made me aſk the reaſon why he pon-
dered ſo much upon it ? To which he
replied, 'Me ſee a boat like this come
to a place in my nation."   And by the
further tokens he gave me, I came to
underſtaud, that the boat was driven in
by a ſtorm.   It preſently came into
my mind that this muſt be ſome Euro-
pean boat that was forced in there by
ſtreſs of weather, after the loſs of the
ſhip ; which put me upon an enquiry,
what ſort of a boat this was, and who
came with it ? he told me they were

white men who came in the boat, and
they were 16 in number; that they
were all alive, and that his country
was very kind to them : upon which it
came into my thot's that thefe muft be
the crew that belonged to the fhip that
was caft away upon my ifland, who
rather than be devoured in the ocean,
had committed themfelves to providence, and confequently were drove a-
fhore among the wild Indians The
notions I had of the cruelty of the favages, made me afk Friday feveral o-
ther queftions concerning them. He
told me he was very certain they ftill
lived there, and were well treated. I
afked him how it came to pafs that
they did not kill them and eat them.
as they do one another ? His aufw.r
was in broken Englifh, ' That they
made friends with them.' He further
added, 'That neither this nation, nor
any other nation that he knew of, ever
eat their fellow creatures, but fuch
whom their law of arms allowed to be
devoured : and they were only thofe

whofe misfortune it was to be prifoners of war.

Some time after this, my man and I went up to the top of a very high hill on the eaft fide of the ifland, from whence I had once feen the continent of America : I could not immediately tell what was the matter, for Friday on a fudden fell to dancing & jumping, as he had been mad, I afked him the reafon of his joy : " O, fays he, I fee iny country, and the very place where the white men live together." Upon which I could not help thinking, but that if he could by any means get home, he would forget all I had done for him, and perhaps bring his countrymen into my ifland to deftroy me : but to my fhame I fpeak it, my jealoufy was very ill grounded : and as I found afterwards, would freely have loft his life, rather than have left me, or done me the leaft injury.

Soon after this, I afked him, if he had not a defire to go into his own country ? His anfwer was, " He loved is own country very well, but would not go without me." Says I, Friday, what shall I do there? He answered you'l do a great deal of good there: you'l learn them to live good lives, and make all the wild men both tame and sober," Alas! says I, Friday, what you say is out of my power: I am not able to make them what you mention, nor will I venture myself among them; no, you shall go yourself, and leave me alone as I was before I saved your life.

Never was any poor innocent creature more thunderstruck than Friday was at these words, especially when I told him he should be at liberty to go as soon as the boat was ready to carry him. This put him into a greater agony yet, desiring me to kill him; "For said he, I had much rather die than lose so good a friend, and so kind a master." When he spake this, the tears ran down his cheeks so plentifully, that I had much ado to refrain from weeping myself; I was forced to comfort him in the best manner I could, telling him; "if he was willing to stay with me, I would never part with him as long as I lived."

In short, the fellows honesty and sincere behaviour, soon convinced me of the unreasonableness of my jealousy, and Friday became more dear to me than ever. Indeed I thought, that if ever I could get to the continent, and join those white men Friday had mentioned, it might be a means to further my return into my native country.

In order to this Friday and I went into the woods to look out a large tree to build a canoe; which with much difficulty, we effected in about 6 weeks time, and with much trouble and pains got her into the water. I was very much rejoiced at launching this little man of war which Friday managed with great dexterity, and assured me it was in all points large enough to carry us over, and that if I thought proper, he was ready to venture with me.

I liked the poor fellow's honest proposal, but at the same time I thought if I could procure a mast and a sail, it

wonld be better; which with the greateſt difficulty imaginable, in about 3
months time, I made a ſhift to patch
together ; and, after that too, I had
my man Friday to inſtruct in the art of
navigation which before he had not the
leaſt notion of.

I was now entered on the twenty-
ſeventh year of my reign, or rather
of my captivity, and kept the anniver-
ſary of my landing with greater ſolem-
nity than ever, having received ſuch
repeated ſignals of divine favour in my
deliverance, preſervation and proſpe-
rity.

I now wanted for nothing, and yet
my mind was ſtill intent upon my deliverance ; and in truth, I had a
ſtrong impreſſion upon me, that I ſhould
not be another year in the iſland : yet
I ſtill continued my huſbandry, and
made the neceſſary preparations for my
future ſubſiſtence. The rainy ſeaſon
coming on, we were forced to continue
for the moſt part within doors, having
firſt made all neceſſary preparations
for the ſecurity and ſafety of my new

boat, till the months of November and
December, at which time I was fully
determined to fail over to the continent : and no fooner did it begin to
draw near, but I began to make preparations for my intended expedition ;
and, in a fortnight's time, I propofed
to open my little dock, and let out
the boat for that purpofe.

One morning, as I was bufy in making preparations for my voyage, Friday, whom I had fent to the fealide to
look for a turtle, came running in a
terrible fright ; fays he, " I have bad
news, yonder is three or four canoes
upon the coaft : and they come to look
for poor Friday, and will eat me as
well as you : and therefore we muft
refolve to fight for our lives. Says
Friday, trembling, Me will fight as
well as I can, but I am afraid they are
too many in number for us ; but I will
obey your orders, and lofe the laft drop
of my blood for you."

Without further difputes, we fell to
loading our arms, and making every
thing ready for the onfet ; when we

had double loaded them, and put every thing in the beſt poſture that could be, I took my perſpective glaſs, and went up to the top of a hill to try what I could diſcover : and I ſoon perceived there were 19 ſavageſs and three priſoners, which I concluded by their manner of acting were to be devoured.

The diſmal and inhuman ſpectacle filled me with the utmoſt horror and deteſtation, and more ſo, becauſe I ſaw a white man, which by their actions and preparations, I found was to be the next ſacrifice : this made me make all the ſpeed I could, being fully determined to deliver him or periſh in the attempt : and ſo I gave Friday orders to follow, and to do every thing that he ſaw me do. When we came to a proper diſtance, undiſcovered, I gave the word to Friday to fire, as I did the very ſame moment. We took our aim ſo well, that between us we killed 4 and wounded three or four more. No man can imagine the conſternation and confuſion theſe ſavages were in, upon this unexpected accident

However not to give them any res-
pite, we took up some other arms, &
let fly upon them a secoud time, killed two more of them and wounded several others : which so added to their
confusion' that they ran yelling and
screaming about like mad creatures.
Says I, "Friday, take the charged mus-
ket, and follow me : So, shewing
ourselves to them, & at the same time
giving a great shout, we went immediately to the victim, and directly cut
the bands from off his hands and legs,
and lifting him up, I asked him in the
Portuguese language, what he was.
He told me in Latin he was a Spaniard, and a Christian : and after returning the best acknowledgments he
could for his deliverance he was about
to give me an account of his misfortunes : but I prevented him, telling
him that would be better another time,
and further said Signior, we will talk
afterwards, but now our business is
fighting. I gave him a dram and a
piece of bread to refresh himself, and

then gave him a sword and a piftol,
and bid him do what he could ; and to
give the man his due, no one could behave himfelf with greater courage. In
fhort we fo managed the matter, of
2 1 favages, not above 3 or 4 got into
one of their canoes, and thofe I was
refolved to purfue and endeavour to
deftroy too, if poffible : accordingly I
leaped into one of their canoes, ordering Friday to follow me : but I was no
fooner got in, but I faw another poor
creature bound hand and foot for the
flaughter, I prefently helped him up,
but he was fo faint and weak, that he
could neither ftand nor fpeak, but
groaned fadly, thinking he was now
facrificed ; I had Friday fpeak to him,
and affure him of his deliverance.-----
When he was a little recovered, and
fat up in the boat, and Friday began
to hear him fpeak, and had looked upon him more fully, you cannot imagine the poor fellow's tranfport ; at
length, when he had a little recovered himfelf, he told me that the perfon

was his father; and in truth, he gave such uncommon testimonies of his duty and affection, that I must needs own I was very much affected with it.

In short with a great deal of difficulty we got both the Spaniard and Friday's father home to my castle, where I made them an handsome tent and treated them in the best manner my circumstances would allow. And thus like an absolute king, I governed my little dominions, and finding that my new subjects were very weak, I ordered Friday to kill one of my kids and stewed and boiled the flesh, and made them some very good broth, and dined with them myself. I then ordered Friday to go to the field of battle, and fetch home the arms; and then I bid Friday ask his father, if he thought it possible for those savages to outride the storm? or if they got home, whether he thought they would not return in great numbers, and endeavour to destroy us? His answer was, that if they did reach their own country, which he scarcely thought possible, yet the strange-nefs of their being attacked would certainly make them tell their people, that they were deftroyed by thunder and lightning, and whoever went into the ifland would certainly be deftroyed by the hands of the gods, and not of man; and that the ifland was inchanted; and that the gods fent fire from above to deftroy all thofe that fhould prefume to land in it.

This account having freed me of my apprehenfions, and no canoes appearing, I refolved to purfue my intended voyage: Friday's father having affured me I might depend upon good ufage from the people of his country. As to the Spaniard, I afked him his opinion, he told me they were 14 that were caft upon the ifland, and that they had good underftanding with the Indians, but were in want of neceffaries for the fupport of human life, and if I thought proper he and the old favage would go over firft, and fettle all matters in order to our reception: and at the fame time, he told me, they would all fwear fidelity to me, & own me as their leader.

Upon these assurances, I resolved to send them over: but when every thing was ready, the Spaniard started this material objection: you know, Sir, says he, I know the length of your stock, and though you may have enough for us that are now with you, yet when you enlarge your family, I am sensible it can never be sufficient to support us long, and therefore my advice is, to wait another harvest, and in the mean time to prepare as much ground as possible, whereby we may have provisions sufficient to carry on our design. This advice I liked extremely, and from that moment I always esteemed the Spaniard, and made him privy councellor on all occasions. We all four went to work, and prepared as much ground as would sow 22 bushel of barley, and 16 of rice, was all the seed we had to spare: and at the same time, I took all the care imaginable to increase & preserve my goats, by shooting the wild dams, & taking the young kids, and putting them into inclosures: and took such other measures, that by

the bleffing of God upon our induftry
after harveft we had provifions to vict-
ual a ship for any part of America.

The principal occafion being thus
anfwered, I gave my two ambaffadors,
a mufket each, with 8 charges of powder and ball, with provifions for the
expedition, and away I fent them.
They had not been gone a fortnight,
but I began to be impatient for their
return, whilft my thoughts were thus
taken up with the expectation of them,
a very ftrange accident happened,
which was firft difcovered by my man
Friday, who one morning came running to me, crying out, they are come,
they are come ; upon which I jumped
from my bed, and looking towards the
fea, I immediatly perceived a boat a
league and a half's diftance, ftanding
directly in for the fhore. I foon found
they were none of my company I expected, for by the help of my glafs, I
found this boat muft belong to fome
fhip, which by cafting my eyes about,
I plainly difcovered lying at anchor, at
fome diftance at fea, which, by the

fashion of her long boat, &c. I concluded muſt be an Engliſh veſſel.

Great was my tranſports upon this
unexpected fight, which brought in my
mind freſh notions of deliverance : &
yet I had ſome cautionary thoughts
which I confeſs were of uſe to me afterwards. It was not long before I
ſaw the boat reach the ſhore, and then
I was fully convinced that they were
Engliſh : I ſaw four of them leap upon
the ſnore, and took three out of them
that looked like priſoners : who I obſerved made paſſionate geſtures of in-

treaty ; & not knowing what the meaning might beckoned to Friday, who
was near me, to go to the top of the
mountain and make what diſcoveries
he could, who in a little time returned
back, " O ! ſays he, Maſter, you ſee
Engliſhman eat mans as well as ſavages." But this I ſoon convinced him to
the contrary ; and yet I could not help
thinking, but there muſt be ſomething
very barbarous in hand. I could not
perceive that they had any fire arms,
but rather that they were preparing to
kill their three companions with their
ſwords ; and now it was I lamented my
want of powder to preſerve them.
However, to my great ſatisfaction, I
found that they turned them up into
the deſolate iſland, as they thought to
be either ſtarved or devoured by wild
beaſts, & then rambled about the wood
to make obſervations till the tide was
gone, and the boat aground.

In ſhort, I conſidered what ſort of
men I had now to deal with, and therefore reſolved to act with all the caution
imaginable, and ſo concluded it was

beſt not to make any attempt till it grew dark : but the day being exceſ five hot, I concluded the ſailors were in courſe laid in the ſhade to ſleep, & perceiving the three poor diſconſolate creatures ſitting under a tree at ſome ſmall diſtance from me, I made no more to do, but went up to them, aſking them in the Spaniſh tongue, " What they were." At which they ſtarted up, and being ſurpriſed at the oddneſs of my dreſs, they began to avoid me, but I called to them in Engliſh, not to be afraid, for you have a friend nearer to you than you expect, tell me your condition, and if it be in my power, I will ſerve you faithfully. 'Sir, ſays one of them, the ſtory is too long at preſent, I was maſter of a ſhip, that lies yonder at anchor, my men have mutinied, and it is a favour they have put this paſſenger, my mate and I, on ſhore on this iſland, without murdering us, tho' we have no proſpect, but to periſh here for want of the neceſſaries of life. Says I, have they any fire arms ? only two fuzees, replied he, &

one of them is now left in the boat, &
if the two desperate rogues that are
with them could be taken, I am pretty
well assured, the rest would return to
their duty. Well said I, let us retire
a little farther under the covering of
the wood and we would talk further;
and there it was I made several condi-
tions with them, which they very
gratefully and honestly performed.'

It was not long before we came to a
resolution to go and attack the villains:
the two men fired upon them and killed
one of the captain's greatest enemies,
and wounded another, the rest cried
for mercy, which was granted them
upon condition they would swear to be
true to him, in helping him to recover his ship, which they all promised
to do in the most solemn manner; however, I advised the captain to keep
them bound, and then our next care
was to secure the boat, without which
it was impossible to reach the ship. To
shorten the relation as much as possible,
we koncerted all our measures so well,

that at laft the fhip was recovered according to our wifh, and now their remained nothing but the difpofal of the
prifoners, the moft dangerous of which
we refolved to leave on the ifland. I
gave them arms, and all the neceffaries I had in my caftle, and telling
them all my whole ftory, I charged them
to be kind to the Spaniards that I had
fent for over. They promifed me very fair, and fo I informed them of every thing neceffary for their fubfiftance :
fo taking with me my man Friday, my
money, my parrot, &c. I went on board,
where the captain treated me as his
deliverer, and behaved himfelf to me
with the utmoft gratitude and civility.
Upon the 12th of December 1687, we
fet fail, and landed in England the 11
of June, 1688, after I had been abfent
from my native country upwards of 35
years.

After my arrival, and I had a little
refrefhed myfelf, I began to enquire
into the ftate of my affairs. I found
my firft captains widow alive, but in
very mean circumftances. Soon after

I went into Yorkshire, where I found
my family in general either dead or
lost, so that I knew no where to find
them. I found that there was no provision made for me, upon which I took
my man Friday, and went to Lisbon,
in order to find out my Portugueze
captain, who took me on board on the
coast of Africa, and to learn from him
what was become of my plantation at
the Brazils. According to my wish,
after some search, I found him out,
who gave me a satisfactory account of
all matters, more particularly of my
plantation in the Brazils, which had
been so honestly managed in my absence
that beyond my expectation, I found
myself worth 40,000l. with which as soon
as possible, I resolved to make the best
of my way to England; and by the advice of the captain I was persuaded to
go by land, which had like to have
proved fatal to me, and all that were
of my company ; for the snows being
fallen, the wolves and bears were driven out of the woods and though we
were more than 20 of us together, they

set upon us several times, and indeed, it was not without the greatest hazard and difficulty we preserved ourselves from being devoured, the particular relation of which would be too long to trouble you with.

In our further passage thro' France we met with nothing uncommon or remarkable : we got safe to Paris, and after a short stay there, we went to Calais, and landed at Dover the 14th day of January, in a very cold season.

When I came to London, I found my bills of exchange all arrived, and the money ready to be paid at sight, which when I had received, it came into my mind to return to Lisbon, and from thence to the Brasils, to look after the plantation ; but upon second thoughts, I thought it proper to write to my correspondent at Lisbon, and desire his advice and assistance, who readily gave me his promise to do all he could for me ; and in truth, as I afterwards found, he acquitted himself to me in every particular, with the greatest judgment and integrity.

In short, he sold my estate for me to the best advantage, and remitted to me for it bills for 320 pieces of eight, a sum much greater than I expected. And now I began to think it high time to settle myself, providence having made such a plentiful provision for me, that I wanted nothing to make myself as happy as I could wish.

Having cast my anchor, and for the present bid adieu to all foreign adventures, I had no other care or concern upon me, but the education of my brother's two sons: one of them I bred a gentleman, and the other I bred an able sailor; and soon afterwards married a virtuous young gentlewoman of a good family, by whom I had two sons and a daughter, but she dying, I grew disconsolate and melancholy, and at the instigation of my nephew, resolved I would once more make a voyage to the East Indies, which I did in the year 1694, and in my passage visited my island.

ADVENTURES

OF

ROBINSON CRUSOE.

MY new kingdom ran continually in my mind, and took up my thot's
both day and night, insomuch that my
wife took notice of it, and would often
ask me the reason of my extraordinary
thoughtfulness, supposing my marri-
age with her might be the cause. Her
tender expressions, together with the
concern I had for the preservation of
my family, brought me to a resolution
to settle myself in some fixed way of
living, accordingly I bought a little
farm in Bedfordshire, and soon provided me a stock with all other implements fit to manage it to the best advantage. In this rural retirement, I
began to think I was as happy as I could
wish, when, on a sudden, all my hap-
piness was destroyed by the unexpected

death of my wife.

Her death gave me a sort of contempt of the world, and filled me with different thoughts and inclinations. My country life grew burdensome to me, and in short, I left my farm, and left off house keeping, and in a few months after, returned to London; but there I could find nothing to entertain me, and divert my melancholy. It was now the beginning of the year 1693, when my nephew whom I had bred up to the sea, was returned from his voyage, the captain of the ship he went out in, who coming to me one morning, told me it was proposed to him by some merchants to make a voyage to the East Indies, and if I would go he would undertake to land me upon my island, that I might have an opportunity to enquire into the state of my new kingdom.

Just before he came to me, it came into my thoughts to get a patent, and fill up my island with inhabitants; 'What devil, said I, sent you hither with this message?' and though I liked the

motion, yet I would not let him know
it at first : however after a little pause.
I told him, if he would set me down,
and call for me at his return, I would
certainly go with him. As to calling
for me as he came back, he told me it
was impractible : " But says he I will
tell you what you can do, we may put
a sloop ready framed on board, which
may be easily put together at any time,
and so I might return with pleasure"
I was not long in forming my resolution ; but contrary to the advice of all
my friends, I was fully determined to
undertake the voyage : and in order to
it, I made my will, and put all my affairs in the best posture I could possible, and so with my trusty servant, Friday, in the beginning of January,
1694, I went on board, and took with
me several artificers, with a good cargo for the better stocking of my island.

We had not been long out at sea,
but we were overtaken by a storm,
which drove us upon the coast of Ire-
land, as far as Galway, where we were
obliged to stay no days for a wind : on-

the 5th of February the wind present-
ed, and we had a very good gale for
several days. On the 20th in the evening, the mate called out that he saw
a flash of fire, and heard a gun, upon
which we all run to the quarter deck,
from whence, at a distance, we saw a
terrible fire, which from our reckon-
ing, we concluded could be no other
than a ship that had taken fire at sea,
and that it could not be far off, by the
report of the guns, which we heard
several times. We made to it with all
our sail, and soon perceived it was a
great ship burning in the midst of the
sea; I immediately ordered five guns
to be fired, that the poor people might
perceive that there was deliverance at
hand, who consequently might endan-
ger their lives in their boats, nor was
it long before the ship blew up.

We hung out our lanthorns, and a-
bout eight in the morning when it began to be light, we saw **two** boats making towards us, so we made a signal
to them to come on board, and took
them up, being men, women, and chil-

dren, in all fixty four. We found it was a French fhip of 400 tons, coming from Canada, and that by the negligence of the fteerfman, it was fet on fire in the fterrage : and that in all probability, if providence had not fent us to their affiftance, they had every foul perifhed.

Never people certainly was fo overjoyed as thefe poor wretches were. Among the paffengers, there were two priefts, an old one, and a young one : the old one was a ftupid old fellow, but the young one was a very modeft gentleman. After their furprtfe was pretty well over, and they had been refrefhed in the beft manner our fhip would allow, the next morning the captain and one of the priefts defired defired to fpeak with me, and offered us the money and jewels they had faved, which I refufed, telling them, our bufinefs was to fave them not to plunder them: they told us, that then all that they had to defire of ns, was to fet them on fhore fomewhere in our paffage. As to landing, we told them that being bound to the Eaſt Indies, we could not do that, without changing our courſe, and that we could not juſtify, but we would carry them till we met with ſome ſhip bound either to England or France, that would take them on board; however, our proviſions beginning to fall ſhort, we reſolved to land them at Newfoundland, which was not much out of our way: and accordingly as we propoſed, in about a week's time, we came to the banks of Newfoundland, where they hired a bark to carry them to France, all but the young prieſt, who choſe to go with us, and two or three of the ſailors.

Now, directing our courſe to the S.S.E. about twenty days after, we met with another adventure that gave us a freſh opportunity to exerciſe our humanity. In the lattitude of 27, we ſaw a ſail bearing towards us, that had loſt all her maſts, and firing a gun in token of diſtreſs, the wind being at N. we ſoon came to ſpeak with her, and found her to be a ſhip of Briſtol, bound home from Barbadoes, that had been driven out of the road by a furious hurricane. They had been toffed about the fea for feveral days, and were almoft ftarved for want of provifions, having eaten nothing for eleven days.

In this fhip, there were three paf-fengers, a gentlewoman, her fon, and a maid fervant : thefe we found in the moft miferable condition that can be imagined. The woman died, and it was not without the greateft care and difficulty that we preferved the young man and the maid, whom, at their ear-neft entreaty, after we had fupplied the fhip with what we could fpare, we took on board our own fhip. We were now in the lattitude of 19 ; but, paffing by fome little incidents, I fhall relate what is moft remarkable, rela-ting to my little kingdom, to which I was now drawing nigh. It was with no fmall trouble, that we got to the fouth fide of my ifland, however, at laft we came to anchor at the mouth of the little creek, and then I faw my old caftle, and knew perfectly where I was.

When I was certain of the place, I called to Friday, and asked him if he knew where he was? the fellow who knew the place as well as myself, replied with a great deal of joy and pleasure, I know very well where we are; yonder is our old castle, and pointing to the hill, I see says he, a great many men. When the English antient was spread, and we had fired three guns, to let them know we were friends I hung out the white flag, and so with the young friar, and my man Friday, I went on shore, and who should I see, the very first man, but the Spaniard whose life I had saved; and Friday who saw his father at a distance, ran to him with all the joy imaginable, and embraced him with extreme tenderness.

It was the 10th of April, that I set my foot on shore the second time, when my faithful Spaniard, accompanied with one more, came up to me; he did not know me at first; but when I hinted to him who I was, no man can exprefs, nor behave himfelf with greater gratitude. He took me by the hand, and afked me if I would not go and take poffeffion of my old habitation, where I found they had made a confiderable improvement. I afked him feveral queftions, and he as readily anfwered me, telling me withal what ftrange confufion they had had with the Englifhmen, who defigned to have murdered them. while we were talking, the man whom he had fent, returned with 11 more. Thefe faid he are fon e of thofe who owe their lives to your goodnefs. And after he had made them fenfible who I was, they all faluted me in a very graceful manner.

WhenI enquired of the Spanirds concerning their manner of living among the favages, they gave me a very deplorable relation of it; adding that they had hardly any hopes of fupport, or of future deliverance. Many were the methods that they took to inftruct the favages, but to no purpofe; for the favages, ignorent as they were, yet would give no ear to the inftructions of thofe who owed them their lives. At the return of their friend, who they thought had been actually devoured, their joy was exceeding great, efpecially when they faw the loaves of bread which I had fent them; but when they heard the errand, and perceived the boat, their tranfports were inexpreffible. This was the account I had from them. And now it follows I fhould inform the reader what I did for them, and in what condition I left them.

As it was generally agreed that they fhould have no more difturbance from the favages, fo I told them, I made this voyage chiefly for their fakes, and I was not come to remove them, but rather to eftablifh and fix them upon the ifland: and for that end, I had brought them all forts of neceffaries & artificers, with other perfons, that would not only add to their number, and confequently to their defence, but would likwife be a mutual help and fupport to them; they were all together when I talked to them after this manner. I afked them one by one, if they had entirely forgot their former animosities, and would engage in the strictest friendship; to which William Atkins replied, they had afflictions anew to make them all sober, and enemies anew to make them all friends; adding withal, that he had most justly deserved the treatment he had received from the Spaniards, and that he was only to blame in the affair; upon which the Spaniards replied, that since Atkins had, upon all occasions, behaved himself so valiently in their common defence, that all that was past should be utterly forgotten: that he should have his arms, and be made the next commander to the governor.

Upon these kind declarations of mutual love and friendship, we concluded to dine together on the morning, which we did in the best order and formality, which the nature of the place would permit, and, after that I distributed to every one of them his portion of the necessaries I had brought over, and then divided the island into three distinct colonies, making my old habita-

tion the metropolis, which the Spaniards inhabited.

The young man whofe mother was
ftarved to death, as before mentioned,
and the maid, who was indeed a very
pious, virtuous young women, feeing
the good difpofition of affairs, dropp-
ed their refolution of going to the Eaft
Indies, and both defired I would permit
them to ftay upon the ifland, and
enter them among my fubjects, the
Englifhmen, which I readily agreed to,
where they lived comfortably ; and
the young woman was afterwards married.

When we came to the Englifhmen I
firft put them in mind, that I had done
every thing for them that was needful,
in order to their future prefervation in
this life, and now my only concern was
the prfervation of their fouls eternally,
I afked them concerning their manner
of living with the favage women, adding, how fcandalous it was to live in
fuch an open and continued courfe of
adultary. To which Atkins replied,

that he believed the savage women
they lived with to be the most innocent
women in the world, and they would
never forsake them : and, to confirm
to me that they were sincere, he told
me, if there was a clergyman in the
ship, they would be married to them
with all their hearts. I told them there
was a clergyman in the ship, and advised them to go and consult the women, and I would take care to have
the ceremony performed to-morrow
morning in due form : which they all
agreed to, aad so the thing was accordingly done to their mutual satisfaction.

In short, the men instructed their
wives as well as they could, in the nature of the thing they were going a-
bout ; and laid them down as far as
their capacities would allow, some general heads of the Christian religion ;
especially Atkins. who, though he had
been by far the most currupt, & vicious,
yet his education had been, by far, better than any of the rest. After the
young priest had asked them several
questions, and they had promised to

amend their lives, and to uſe their utmoſt endeavours to make their wives
Chriſtians, he married them ; which
was not more to my ſatisfaction, than
to that of the Engliſhmen themſelves,
and indeed was attended with all the
good conſequences that could be expected.

The affairs of the iſland being thus
ſettled, I was preparing every thing
for going on board, when the young
man, whoſe mother had been ſtarved,
as is before mentioned, came to me,
ſaying, as he underſtood there was a
clergyman on board, that had married the Engliſhman and the ſavages, he
had a match to propoſe between two
Chriſtians, which he deſired might be
finiſhed before I went. At firſt, I tho't
it might be between himſelf and his
mothers maid, and began to give him
ſome advice to the contrary. Upon
which he told me I was miſtaken ; he
had nothing to aſk of me for his part,
but a ſmall parcel of ground for a plantation, a ſervant or two, and a few
neceſſaries : and that I would not be

unmindful of him when I came to England ; but as for the match I am to propose to you, it is between the Englishman you call Jack of all trades, and the maid Susan.

I was agreeably surprised at the mentioning this match which was very suitable ; the fellow being a very active industrious man, and the woman a discreet, neat, cleanly house wife, and so the match was concluded, and they were married the same day. As to their sharing out the land, I left it to William Atkins, who indeed discharged the trust with great fidelity.   As to their laws and government, I advised them earnestly to love one another, & to make what further by laws they should think proper for their general good and benefit.

At our return, we called to Atkin's house, where we found the new married woman in a close conference with Atkin's wife, who had been baptized. Says Atkins, when God has sinners to reconcile to himself, he is never without an instructor : for this young woman, whom Providence has sent among us, has sense and religion enough to convert a whole island of savages. The young woman blushed and was going to rise, but I bid her sit still, telling her I hoped God would bless her good endavours, and so, taking out of my pocket a Bible, I gave it to Atkins, which he received with the greatest marks of gratitude and satisfaction : & so, after many religious discourses, I desired the young woman to give me the best account she could of the anguish she felt, when she was starving to death in the ship, which she did in terms very moving and pathetic.

And now, having disposed every thing in the island in the best manner possible, and given the people assurances that I would always have them in my thoughts, and would be sure to send them sufficient supplies, as often as I had an opportunity. Upon the 1st of May 1695, I set sail for the Brasils. But the next day we were becalmed, and looking towards the N N E. of the island, we could perceive something at sea looking very black, upon which the mate going up to the shrouds, and taking a view with a prospective glass, cried out, It was an army : an army, says I, you fool ! how can that be ? Nay sir, says he, do not be in a passion ; for I can assure you, it is not only an army but a fleet too, and they are making all speed they can towards us.

As they came nearer towards us, they seemed to be very much surprised at the sight of the ship, not knowing what to make of us, and our men being unwilling they should come too near us, made signs to them to keep off, which they did ; but as they retired, they let fly several arrows, by which one of our men was wounded.

In a little time they had the courage to come so near us that they could hear us speak ; upon which I ordered Friday to call to them, to know what they would have, upon which they poured a whole cloud of arrows upon him, seven of which went through his body, and so I had my faithful servant,

and my moft affectionate companion in
all my affliction and folitude.   I was fo
enraged at the death of poor Friday,
that I ordered the gunners to load with
fmall fhot, and immediately give them
a broadfide, which they did fo effectually, that 12 or 14 of their canoes were
overfet, and the reft fo frightened,
that away they flew with all the fpeed

they could; but our men took one poor wretch, about an hour afterwards, as he was swimming for his life; but the creature was so stubborn and surly, that I could not prevail with him either to eat or drink, upon which I ordered them to throw him into the sea, by which means, after we had taken him the second time, he came so far to himself, that he let us know that they were going with their king to fight a great battle; and when we asked him what made them come to us, and shoot at us? all the answer he could make us was, that they only came to wonder at us. Poor Friday was buried with all the pomp and decency our circumstances would allow. And now, having a fair wind, we made the best of our way to the Brasils, and in a few days came to an anchor in the bay of All Saints. With some difficulty I got on shore with part of my cargo, and having fitted out a vessel with provisions for my island, and settled several letters with my correspondent, we set sail for the East Indies.

We ſailed from the Brazils and made directly to the Cape of Good-Hope, having a tolerable good voyage, ſteering for the moſt part S. E. At the Cape we only took in freſh water, and then ſailed directly for the coaſt of Coromandel. The firſt place we touched at, was the iſland of Madagaſcar, where, though the people are fierce and treacherous, yet they treated us woll, and gave us commodities. I made it my chief buſineſs to go on ſhore as often as I could, to make obſervations; and indeed, the people traded with us with much ſeeming civility.

We put to ſea again, being reſolved to put into the firſt trading port we came near. After ſome days ſail, we came within ſight of ſhore, and ſtanding in, a boat came off to us, with an old Portugueze pilot on board, who offering us his ſervice, we very gladly accepted it, and ſent the boat back again: in ſhort the old man went with us, and as we ſailed along, I aſked him if there were no pyrates in thoſe ſeas? he told me, he had not heard of any that had been in those seas for many years, except one that was seen in the bay of Siam, about a month ago; nor was she built for a runner neither, but only a ship that the men had run away with, the captain having been murdered by the Mallayans, and I can tell you this, by some Dutchmen that came near them the other day, in the river Cambodia, had laid their hands upon them, and would have hanged every one of the rogues upon the yard arm without any further ceremony.

Being sensible that this old pilot could do us no harm, I told him how cases stood with us, and desired him to carry us to Nanquin.

We arrived at Nanquin, when to our great joy, we sold our vessel to a merchant of Japan, and afterwards travelled with a large caravan, with many difficulties in our journey, through China, Siberia, and Muscovy, and arrived at London on the 10th of January, 1705, having been absent from England, this last time, ten years, and nine months. And now resolving to harrass myself no more, I am preparing for a longer journey than all those; for I have lived seventy-two years, chequered with surprising variety, and have been taught sufficiently the value of retirement, and the blessing of ending my days in peace, and in the true worship of my Almighty deliverer.

F I N I S.

www.ingramcontent.com/pod-product-compliance
Lightning Source LLC
Chambersburg PA
CBHW020405030726
47496CB00007B/2314